Too Much Tinsel
Amy Wolf

Contents

1. Front Matter — 1
2. 1940's Slang — 3
3. Characters — 6
4. An Unexpected Visit — 9
5. The Reading of the Will — 12
6. One of Three — 15
7. Lady Shamus — 18
8. The Blue Egg — 24
9. Mrs. Felize Pays a Visit — 34
10. On the Case — 38
11. A Love Triangle—Or Not? — 44
12. The Commissary — 49
13. Good Cop — 55
14. The Women — 67
15. Mrs. Felize Steps Out — 73
16. Number Three — 79
17. The Lion Roars — 88
18. Manly's Boys — 95

19.	Death on the Backlot	98
20.	Don't Screw with a Studio	103
21.	Ma Chimes In	109
22.	Dancing the Night Away	118
23.	The Lonely Dragon	126
24.	Foxing Around	130
25.	Ask an Expert	134
26.	First We Kill All the Lawyers	139
27.	The Yachting Life	144
28.	Seasick	151
29.	Next, Kill All the Lawyers	153
30.	A Kindred Soul	160
31.	Swingin' at the Grove	164
32.	Howie Comes Clean	172
33.	Wescott and Spencer	180
34.	Anatomy of a Shooting	189
35.	Eating at the Hat	193
36.	The Hollywood Hills	197
37.	Among the Whispering Palms	201
38.	The Premiere	214
39.	Whodunit?	219
40.	A Yes, a No, and a Maybe	227
41.	Glamor Is What She Sells	233
42.	Barbarians at the Gate	240

43. Hollywood Magic					245

Chapter 1
Front Matter

This is a work of fiction. Similarities to real people, places, or events are entirely coincidental.

TOO MUCH TINSEL

Book 1 of Flames and Fame

First edition January 2024

Copyright © 2024 Amy Wolf

Written by Amy Wolf

Find out more about the author and upcoming books online at:

https://amy-wolf.com

https://lonewolfpress.com

https://twitter.com/@AmyWolf_Author

https://www.facebook.com/profile.php?id=100088956518783

"That's pictures, baby."

—someone to Frank Capra

Acknowledgments:

Tim Whittome: Proofreader.

Cover Illustration: Paramita Creative.

Dedication:

This book is dedicated to the memory of my mom, Sylvia Faith Wolf (1938–2020), our beloved "Did."

I miss her every day.

And Pat Johnson, a Hollywood heavy.

Ken Kenyon, 20th Century Fox head librarian extraordinaire.

Chapter 2
1940's Slang

4 0's Slang

"Aces" – good

"Ameche" – telephone (after actor Don Ameche, who starred in the movie *The Story of Alexander Graham Bell*)

"Bananas" or "Goofy" – insane

"bet a dollar to a Canadian dime" – I'm sure

"Bird" – a man

"Black-and-white" – LAPD police car

"Blip" or "Ice" or – to kill

"Blow" – leave

"Blue nose" – upper class

"Boffo B.O." – refers to a big box office success

"Bombshell" – a sexy woman

"Boozehounds" – people who drink a lot of alcohol

"Bub" – a term of endearment or casual address, like 'buddy'

"Bull" or "John" – a cop

"Burbank top" – a convertible

"Button man" – a hired killer or gunman

"C-note" – a hundred dollars

"Chintzy" – cheap

"Cooler" or "Icebox" – jail

"Cutter" – a film or sound editor

"Dope" – information

"Dough" "Clams" or "Smacks" – money

"dummied-up" – keep quiet

"Floozy" – a loose woman

"Floperoo" – something that is a flop or failure

"Foxing around" – investigating

"Frau" – Mrs.

"Gat" or "Heat" – a gun or pistol

"Grand" – a thousand dollars

"Harpo" – silent or mute, referring to Harpo Marx, known for his silent role in the Marx Brothers films

"Heat" or "Iron" – gun

"High society" – upper class

"In a jif" – in a jiffy, meaning very quickly

"Jake" – okay or all right

"Jalopy" – a car

"Jeepers" – an expression of surprise.

"Joe" – coffee

"Joint" – a place

"Jonesing" – craving or yearning for something.

"Keep your hush" – keep quiet

"Killer diller" – Something or someone very exciting or impressive

"Knockout" – a sexy woman

"Make" – have sex

"Off the beam" – strange

"Pill" – a bullet

"Pinch" – arrest

"Pictchas" – what studio people call pictures

"Pretty darned" – an emphatic phrase meaning very or extremely

"Pump" – heart

"Put the bite on" – try to extort

"Racket" – illegal business

"Screwy" – odd/eccentric

"Shamus" – private detective

"Shyster" – lawyer

"Squeeze" – blackmail

"Stepping out" – unfaithful

"Swell" – great or excellent.

"Swinging" – trendy, fashionable, or lively

"Take a powder" – to leave or depart

"To print something" – run prints

"Trouble boy" – a gangster

"Two bits" – a quarter of a dollar

"Yellow" – a coward

"Your hush" – silence

Yiddish

"Bupkis" – nothing

"Shmendrik" – an idiot/fool

Chapter 3
Characters

Characters

Nicky Forenza, PI
Errol the Dragon – her partner
Bill Anderson – LAPD
Angelo Forenza -Nicky's Pops
Guiseppe Lombardo – PI
Ma
Matteo Rossi – young guy
Tony & Michael Forenza – Nicky's brothers in the Navy
Brock Powell – Hollywood heartthrob
Carrie Joanford – actress
Catherine Wescott – Oscar-winning actress
Cecil B. DeMille – major producer
Eddie – a gangster
Freida Braun – German bombshell
Heinrich von Heinrich – washed-up director
Hugh Hughley – eccentric billionaire/producer

Ingrid Johansson – Swedish actress
Larry Felize – gaffer
Lloyd Richardson – minor Mammoth player
Meir Lenski – head of Mammoth Studios
Mickey McSweeney – director
Milicent Weller – his wife
Mrs. Felize – wife
Nelly Swan – Silents actress
Patrick Magee – editor
Robert Marion – actor
Tommy Manly – 2nd to Lenski
Tony Alexander – grip
Tracy Spenser – actor
Wes Haskell – cameraman/DP
"Wild Billy" – director
William Weller – director
Zuck Adolph – head of Mountain Pictures

Contents

An Unexpected Visit 8
The Reading of the Will 11
One of Three 14
Lady Shamus 17
The Blue Egg 23
Mrs. Felize Pays a Visit 33
On the Case 37
A Love Triangle—Or Not? 43
The Commissary 49
Good Cop 55
The Women 67
Mrs. Felize Steps Out 73

Number Three 79
The Lion Roars 87
Manly's Boys 94
Death on the Backlot 96
Don't Screw with a Studio 101
Ma Chimes In 107
Dancing the Night Away 116
The Lonely Dragon 124
Foxing Around 128
Ask an Expert 132
First We Kill All the Lawyers 137
The Yachting Life 142
Seasick 149
Next, Kill All the Lawyers 151
A Kindred Soul 158
Swingin' at the Grove 162
Howie Comes Clean 170
Wescott and Spencer 178
Anatomy of a Shooting 188
Eating at the Hat 192
The Hollywood Hills 195
Among the Whispering Palms 199
The Premiere 212
Whodunit? 217
A Yes, a No, and a Maybe 224
Glamor Is What She Sells 230
Barbarians at the Gate 237
Hollywood Magic 242

Chapter 4
An Unexpected Visit

November, 1944

I had been through too much to die today.

I searched through my bag for keys to my "bachelor" apartment. My hand brushed against a tumble of objects: lipstick tubes in two shades of red, blush, eye shadow: in my line, a pretty face could open doors. My hand, submerged in fake leather, bumped against something cold and hard. I could picture its color—black. Just as I tugged on the handle, I felt a poke in the middle of my spine.

Just my luck. How had I not heard them?

"Afternoon, Nicky," said one, hemming me in as he turned the key in the lock. "Home kinda early, huh?"

"I didn't expect a welcoming committee."

The goon—a punk in his 20's, cheap checkered suit falling in folds around his thin body—gestured for me to step inside. As if I had a choice. Once I stood in my living room (also the bedroom and tiny kitchen), I turned to face the two hoods. The punk's pal was slightly older and just as cheaply dressed.

These guys need to find a good tailor, I thought, as the older hood pulled his piece.

"C'mon," I said, "no need for the double heat. You got me, fair and square."

The young punk smirked.

"That's right," he growled, "and the boss wants to make sure you don't cause no more trouble."

"Trouble?" I asked, arching an eyebrow. "Just working for a living, boys."

"Yeah," said Hood #2, shoving his iron right in my face. "That's the problem, right there. Mr. Manly wants you gone."

"But . . . doesn't he care about the murders?"

I fluttered my lashes demurely. Thick mascara made them heavy.

"Sure, sure," the hood mumbled, "he just don't want 'em made public. Bad publicity and all that."

I rolled my eyes. With these studio folks, that's all that ever mattered.

"What if I'm discreet?" I asked, now pushed up by his friend against a bare, peeling wall. "I can find the killer and not tell the *Examiner*—"

"Manly don't want no dame nosing around his turf. Him and Lenski can handle it."

"Like they handled Harlow's husband?"

The button man winced. He must have remembered the suicide—and Lenski pocketing evidence.

"I don't like your smart mouth," the gunman growled, his olive skin glistening as he moved his stubbled face near mine.

"Me neither," I said, "but I can't help it. I was born this way."

As his fist hit my stomach, I folded in half. The pain ran through me like the special at Union Station. Then the punk got into the act, pinning my arms above my head. Good thing I still had legs. I used them, four-inch spiked heel extended like a dagger, to kick him hard in the nuts. He went down in segments: first, his scuffed Thom McCann's, then the folds of his oversized suit, and finally, a sharp black fedora which fell over his eyes.

"Why you—" the second hood spat, thumbing the hammer of his .38 Special. Just as cheap as the rest of him.

"Hey," I practically yelled, "would you treat your sister this way?"

"You ain't my sister."

"But I could be." I decided to play the Italian card. "Don't our people have enough grief without us killing each other?"

"I ice guineas all the time."

"But not their wives?" I suggested hopefully.

"The wives are home making dinner and watching the kids. Now his slim finger curved lovingly around the trigger. He shrugged. "I do what I'm told."

"Just like the—"

I was going to say "Blackshirts," but never got the chance. Someone charged through the shut front door, causing a tornado of flying splinters and paint. The visitor saw my predicament, frowned, and crossed arms over his chest.

"Errol!" I called in relief. The hood holding my arms looked over his shoulder: Alas, his last act in life. Bright orange flames licked his body as he fell screaming onto the stained carpet. "Thanks," I told his assailant, clutching my still smarting stomach.

He nodded, unmoving, then placed his bare foot on the punk stretched out before him.

Thank God, I thought, leaning over to grab the bad guy's gun. If Errol hadn't shown up, I would be as dead as the chickens in Goldblatt's window. That day, a lot of things made me feel lucky.

But mostly, the fact that my partner was a dragon.

Chapter 5
The Reading of the Will

*F**our months earlier...*

"WHAT?!" I yelled, nearly scaring the smooth-voiced lawyer out of his tailored suit.

"Mr. Hughley—" the man repeated, surveying me with contempt. Sure, I was far below him in the pecking order of justice, but he didn't have to rub it in. I felt like grabbing one of those law books groaning from the shelf behind me and whacking him over the head. But no—that would mess up his ten-dollar haircut.

"I heard you the first time," I said, pitching my voice low. Feminine wiles didn't work on a shyster like Howie Goldstein. "But why?"

Goldstein shrugged in his high-backed chair. Real leather, I observed. Still, it made him look small.

"Mr. Hughley, as you know, could be somewhat peculiar—"

"That's like saying Hitler is somewhat bad! This is a man . . ." I leaned forward in my low guest chair. Of course, Goldstein must appear bigger. ". . . who stored his own urine in jars! Who never cut his fingernails! Who surrounded himself with Mormons—"

"Pious bastards," Goldstein mumbled. "He left them a fortune."

"I guess," I said, "the Golden Salamander never appeared to you."

"Hmmp." Goldstein set his expression to "calm." "I can't answer for Mr. Hughley. Billionaires have this strange habit of doing just what they want."

"That's the problem!" I cried, digging myself out of my seat. "Why would a rich guy like Hughley refuse to pay my fee? He had me follow that actress—the one with the big—" I curved my hands, making the universal gesture.

"—Jugs," Goldstein finished, now completely unruffled. "Look, it's a quid pro quo. Obey Hughley's last wish and you get paid. Plus—" He scrunched his eyes over parchment as long as the L.A. River. "See it through, and it means twenty-five grand. In cash."

I grabbed onto a bookcase, unable to imagine such a sum. Me, who got twenty-five a day, and if I was lucky, expenses! This huge payoff would mean . . . law school, at last . . . money for Ma to manage the household . . . and the extra for Tony and Michael, so far away overseas . . .

I blinked, bringing Goldstein back into focus.

"Okay," I said, "it's a deal. Did Hughley leave specific instructions?"

"Nope. Just the usual care and feeding. You got kids?"

"I've never been married."

"Lucky you. You play Mama as a girl?"

Memories wafted over me of toy metal trucks and trains.

"More like policeman."

He chuckled.

"Find out what it likes and feed it. What do lizards eat—bugs?"

I shrugged.

"Do I look like a zookeeper?"

His shoulders rose as he laughed again.

"Just make sure it stays alive—or all that dough goes bye-bye."

Even those few C's I earned fair and square.

"I understand," I said, reaching out with both arms to grab a blue oval object. "Goodbye, Mr. Goldstein. If I'm lucky, I'll never see you again."

"That makes two of us."

He tossed his sand-colored fringe in the direction of the door.

"Good luck," he told me. "Don't suppose you care much about that thing, but remember—it's worth a fortune."

It was hard for me to forget the sound of jingling coins—or the crisp feel of bills. Nodding, I let myself out, deciding to head to the office.

Chapter 6
One of Three

There were three—maybe four—dame PI's in the whole state of California, and to my own surprise, I was one of them.

Why? I wondered, stepping from my old Ford into a Hollywood building which should have been demolished, *had I gone along with Guiseppe?* I nodded hello to the telephone girl I the lobby—a real loose screw—and slouched into an elevator just days away from death. As I shot upward with the speed of a baby sloth, I replayed the scene in my head as if a year hadn't passed.

"Nicky, I'm begging," Guiseppe had pleaded while I stood in Ma's lounge in my ridiculous LAPD "uniform": an all-white getup that made me look like a nurse. "Your father—"

I closed my eyes painfully. Yeah, Pops was out in Montana, one of many Italians they'd picked up after Pearl Harbor. As if Pops, with his modest bodega, was Mussolini's henchman! Still, he'd had no choice but to go. If only he'd had been naturalized, this whole nightmare wouldn't have happened. Maybe. I looked over Guiseppe's head straight into blackout curtains.

"Nicky, you're a smart girl! UCLA and everything! Your father was so proud . . ."

Ha! I thought. He'd yelled at operatic volume at the very idea of *his daughter* earning a college degree. After all, no one else in the family had one and they were doing Okay, and wasn't it expensive, and didn't I need to spend my time finding a nice husband?

Instead, I spent my time making money. First as a shopgirl at Woolworth's—fun—then at Lockheed, where I ran a drill press and hefted a metal lunchbox. The pay was amazing—$1.05 an hour!—and it didn't take long to raise the dough for UCLA. For four years, I'd lived at home, studied like a fiend, and left with a formal paper declaring me a B.A. I so desperately wanted—and want—to go to law school, but UCLA didn't have one, leaving just USC. That wasn't going to work. At the University of Spoiled Children, you had to have big bucks to go—*like five grand a year!* That's how I landed at the LAPD, one of the strolling nurses protecting downtown from boozehounds. Silly me. I thought I'd look good on an application.

"Nicky?"

Guiseppe snapped his fingers and my eyes refocused.

"Nicole Sophia Forenza!" Ma yelled from the kitchen, her face obscured by steam. "You show some respect to your elders!"

"What'd I do?" I mumbled.

Guiseppe took a step toward me, his blue-veined hands shaking.

"I don't know who else to turn to. You're a bull, and a good one—"

"Pul-leaze!" I snorted. "I spend most of my time calling for backup. From *real* bulls with *real* guns—"

"That doesn't matter." Guiseppe was breathing so hard I thought he might pass out. "He's after me. Earl Warren. I made the fatal mistake of writing to Italy. And now, just like your dad, they'll come to haul me away!"

"But the President said we're good now. Not enemy aliens."

Guiseppe's mouth twisted.

"California has its own set of rules."

"Like always." I stood there, shaking my head. "Look, Mr. Lombardo, I'm barely a cop, much less a detective. I've never done work like that."

"Your Pops used to say," he answered, "you wanted to go back to school. I-I know it's pricey, but if you take over my practice—"

"I don't even know where to start."

"I have an apprentice. Young guy. Hungry. He can show you the ropes."

"Why not have him take over?"

"Sweet kid, that Matteo. But not much going on upstairs."

To the last, I resisted.

"I don't know, Mr. Lombardo. I mean *me*, a shamus? That wasn't exactly my plan."

Guiseppe grabbed my shoulders.

"It wasn't *my* plan to freeze my culo off in Montana. But you'll learn, Nicky, that's life." He removed his hands. "And being a sleuth can get you places. Put you in solid with school. Please." His dark eyes shone. "I spent ten years building my business. Can't just leave it to die."

I spotted Ma moving up quickly, ready to strike with her ladle.

"Nicole Forenza, you help your father's friend! Anything else would be shameful!"

I'd been beaten. Italian guilt hung over the room like a wraith.

"Okay," I said.

After all, how much worse could it be than playing nursemaid to drunks?

Chapter 7
Lady Shamus

*M*arch, 1943...

As it turned out, a lot worse.

Guiseppe arranged a meeting between me and Matteo, and he was just as described: nice kid; no brains. I followed him up the stairs of another Hollywood building, this one ready for last rites. He bent over to unlock the door of a small office. "Guiseppe Lombardo, PI," the black lettering read. I'd have to change it.

I looked around at the faceless space consisting of cheap furniture and a small mini-icebox. Matteo stood before me, arms crossed.

"So," he started, "you'll need a partner, yes?"

"I don't know," I said honestly. "And even if I did, I doubt I can afford one."

He frowned. We were not, as they say, getting off on the right foot.

"What do you know about foxing around?" he asked.

"Huh? What's in there?" I said, pointing to an inner glass door.

"Mr. Lombardo's office."

"Let's get used to the way things are now—it's *mine*."

He stared moodily at the torn carpet.

"Yeah. You a sleuth or what?"

"More 'what.' I was a cop." I looked him in the eye. "LAPD."

This seemed to earn some respect.

"Aces," he said. "Let's start with getting your license."

"Okay."

"First, you got to get certified."

"What does that mean?"

"Well, you're over eighteen—"

"I'm twenty-eight."

"Right. Now, you got to be of good character."

"That's debatable."

"And you'll need five letters from folks who've known you at least five years. No family."

I sighed.

Did I have that many friends?

"I'll file the bond for you, and the license costs fifty smackers. Here." He shoved a damp wad of bills in my hand. "From Mr. Lombardo."

Amazingly, I managed to find five people who'd put in a good word for me: two UCLA classmates, my supervisor at LAPD, a cop, and Becky, a childhood friend. I stood at the California Bureau of Security and Investigative Services, or BSIS, (which to me, was so much BS), proudly accepting a card declaring me worthy. Since I wasn't, I cornered Matteo back at the office, forcing him to put down his comic book. I was ready to get this thing started.

"First lesson," I announced.

He glanced yearningly at his comic.

"Okay. So Mr. Lombardo tol' me: don't let nothing escape your eye."

I nodded. In this game, that was kind of a given.

"He also said listen to a bird named Holmes: Sometimes a clue is left in the most obvious place."

"That's obvious," I said.

"Look. Mr. Lombardo was hired to fox around on a case about auto juice. Black market. Wanna tag along?"

"Sure," I said, not bothering to take off my coat. "Where do we start?"

Matteo gave me the backstory after we'd boarded a yellow "N" streetcar. It was now late afternoon.

"So, there's this gang," he told me, "stealing gas and selling it. No other heisters come close." I nodded to the beat of wheels on tracks. "Head guy's named Rocco."

"Of course."

"He's a 'made man.' Know what I mean? Very big and very tough."

"Who works for him?"

"Four guys. Sicilian."

I shrugged. That's where Pops came from. Not *all* of us were gangsters.

We hopped off the "N" downtown, Matteo in the lead. We didn't look like detectives: more like a boy and his Ma on an outing. Matteo walked briskly, heading to the outskirts of town which consisted of ramshackle houses. Talk about a rough neighborhood. I saw kids not playing hoops and sticks, but with a tommy gun!

"This way," Matteo whispered. I crept behind in my heels—a poor choice of footwear. He led me to an old rusted, steel door; firmly locked against intruders. Then, he just stood there.

"Well?" I hissed.

Where was the secret entrance?

"Um, this is as far as we got. Mr. Lombardo couldn't find no way in."

I put my head in my hand, careful not to smear makeup.

"We came all this way to stare at a shut door?"

"Yup," he said cheerfully, turning and ready to leave.

"Not so fast," I breathed. This was my first case, and I wanted to catch some crooks. "You carry a gun?" I asked.

"Oh no! Mr. Lombardo—"

I rummaged in my bag, withdrawing my wallet. "Here. Take this. Buy a gat from those kids." He opened his mouth to protest, saw I wasn't kidding, and approached the mini Capones. After a whispered discussion, he dragged back with a revolver. "Hand it over," I ordered, and taken aback by my tone—*from a broad, no less!*—he did as I said. At the LAPD, women didn't carry heat—hell, we were lucky we had a *badge*. Still, I seized the piece, flipped open the cylinder, and spun it. Good news. Full up with six pills. Still clutching the gun, I led Matteo around to what looked like a big warehouse. "Keep your eyes open," I hissed, sidling along a wall as I searched for a back entrance. During his last visit, Lombardo must have been thinking of Warren since I easily spotted a door affixed with a heavy padlock.

"You pick locks?" I asked Matteo.

He looked terrified. *How hard could this be?* From my bag, I fished out a steel nailfile, inserting its point into the keyhole. I was pretty good with my hands having run a drill press at Lockheed. I probed at the padlock, twisting my file carefully. With a last gentle turn, the hasp sprang open!

"Sweet mother Mary," said Matteo, wide-eyed. I could tell he'd never expected a dame to be good at "foxing around." I opened the door a crack, squinting at the one light source: a naked bulb on a chain. Deep in the warehouse interior, I could hear the murmur of men and then the rev of an engine. I made out the silhouette of a Bentley and its impatient driver.

Another big shot, I thought, *too good for wartime rations, and paying through the nose for juice.* An indignity swelled inside me like a too-tight balloon. This town ran on autos and the rich ran the town.

"Matteo," I hissed, turning back, "go find a black and white. Two would be even better."

He nodded, scampering off. Before stepping inside, I threw off my heels. As my eyes adjusted, I saw a huddle of suits. Good thing for me they were busy.

"That's fifty clams," a rough voice demanded, and I heard the shuffle of bills. "Remember who your friends are. We're always here when you need us."

There was a chuckle as I moved in, watching the Bentley drink from a thick hose.

Cops, I thought, *where are they?* L.A. was a big city now, and most major streets had patrols. *Come on, Matteo,* I thought, *no time to lose your nerve!* Then the wide steel door at the front started to grind its way up. *No!* Not only would the driver escape, but I, the shoeless wonder, would be lit up like a Christmas tree!

The door was now half open. If I didn't do something, Rocco and his goons would walk. I gulped, steeling myself. *I could do this.* Stepping out of the shadows, I pointed my heat at the seated men.

"Freeze," I ordered, giving them a good look at the muzzle. They were right between the sites. I addressed a balding man in a dark, outsized suit. From his girth, I knew who he was. "Rocco, this racket stops here. I've got a full load of pills—more than enough for all of you."

I don't know where I got the nerve—me, Miss UCLA, Miss Pretend Cop—holding them all at bay while I clutched my grip with both hands. I fought to keep them steady.

"Who the hell is this broad?" one hood spat, snaking an arm toward his pocket. I fired a round into the corrugated roof. This seemed to get their attention.

"Irons on the floor, boys. Better them than you." With reluctance, my demand was granted by the clank of steel on concrete. Based on the number of guns circling my stockinged feet, I could have opened a shop. "Cops'll be here soon," I bluffed, "so hands in the air and no tricks."

"C'mon, sister," Rocco started, but I wasn't in the mood.

"Keep it buttoned!" I snarled, trying to sound tough. In fact, my heart was beating like Gene Krupa on drums.

Then, a welcome sound echoed from the street: the whine of a nearby siren.

"I'm sending you down, Rocco," I said, "you and this gang of trouble boys. Bring a coat. You'll need it in the cooler."

A swarm of blue swept in, snapping on silver bracelets like they were made by Tiffany. Behind them, I saw Matteo, mouth open in shock.

And that's why the evening *Times* reported: "Lady Shamus Makes Good On First Case."

Guiseppe, probably with Pops by now, would have been so proud.

Chapter 8
The Blue Egg

November, 1944

I slipped a key in the lock, opening the glass door which read, "Nicky Forenza, PI." The reception desk was vacant—the way things were going, I couldn't afford a Matteo. Glad to put down my burden, I took the big blue egg and balanced it in my "In" box.

Now what? I wondered. *What did Hughley have in mind, and how much did he know about this object he'd pulled "from the center of the Earth"?*

I shrugged. For all I knew, the egg was a fake, and Hughley had read too much Verne.

I opened the door to my private office and saw it was a mess. How I'd managed to spew so many papers across such a small space might require its own case. I sat down in a chair which made Goldstein's look like a Louis XIV. He'd probably had them designed by some studio set decorator.

I steepled my fingers and thought. Hughley owed me some C-notes—not to mention the twenty-five grand.

But, I wondered, *what if that dumb egg never hatches?* Then Hughley had screwed me over like all the stars he'd courted. *Just like a man,* I thought. Never tying things up neatly—always leaving a strand behind. I started as my phone rang, picking up the receiver and sneezing from all the dust.

"Nicky Forenza," I said, trying to sound all business. "How can I help you?"

I listened to some woman chatter about my first case: Yeah, I knew all about it. When I hung up, I honestly wondered if I'd ever work again. It wasn't like the good people of L.A. were flocking to my door. Despite that brief spurt of fame.

And so it went . . . for the next three weeks. Brightly-lit meals at Rexall's counter and sleepless nights in my lumpy pull-down bed. At the office, no clients, not even those begging to tail a spouse. Yet . . . *something* piqued my interest, and of all things, it was that damned blue egg!

At first, it had just sat there, precariously balanced against the frame of my "In" Box. Two weeks later, it started to stir, rolling around like a bowling pin.

Was this, I wondered, *some posthumous prank of Hughley's?* A final middle finger before he soared into the void? If he was trying to kid me, he'd sure put in the work.

Day 15, and the egg started to crack with the smallest of sounds. Since I was alone, this was my main source of fun, until on Day 16, the cracks became more jagged, crunching their way across the blue surface.

Early that night, it happened: The cursed thing opened, and a baby lizard crawled out. Christ, was Hughley an oddball! Making it down to the planet's core and all he came back with was a pest you'd find in your garden.

From my desk, I heard a small peep. That meant I had to feed it. I stared down at the small creature lying in its broken shell. It gave me a piteous look with small, round yellow eyes. Bending closer, I noticed four tiny claws with talons and a tail shaped like a spade. Its color was nothing to crow about: just the dull tan of men's shoes. I moved in even more. If I'd been a sob sister, I might have said it was cute, but though I wasn't, it was. A series of peeps escaped its mouth: did lizards even have them, or was that a snout? I shrugged, uncaring, until the little guy made his move by unfurling thin wings.

Hold the phone! *Wings?* I'd heard of flying lizards, so this one must be that kind. At the next pathetic peep, I swung round to my scratched percolator, grabbing a carton of milk. I kept it around for clients who couldn't stomach pure joe.

What could I use to feed it? An eyedropper wasn't included in my office supplies. Still, I was a shamus—and I searched the desk's messy contents. Pleased, I picked up a ballpoint ink refill and emptied out the contents. Grudgingly, I even cleaned it before pouring in some milk.

"Damn!" I yelled, scattering drops over the wood. But the little guy didn't care: When I tipped the improvised bottle, it grabbed it with two front claws and drained it in an instant. "Could eat a horse, huh?" The lizard folded its arms. *Geez!* Touchy. I kept giving it milk until, with a drunk expression, it rolled onto its back.

"Brrrp!" it said.

"Hey, manners, bub!"

Now what?

Reluctantly, I shoved the thing in my coat, deciding to take it to my joint. What else could I do? With twenty-five G's plus change on the line, I would not let this lizard come to harm. I walked down Hollywood Boulevard, past the boozehounds and flashing neon. It was like living in Reno—*inside* a casino. But my wallet was thin and the Proctor, with its "bachelor" apartments, was all I could swing. In the lobby, I nodded to the girl, then creaked up the ancient elevator to unlock my door. My coat now made so much noise it could have been nabbed for disturbing the peace.

"Swell," I said, swinging open my mini-icebox to free some more milk. Taking the scaly noisemaker with me, I went into my closet-sized bathroom to fetch a *real* eyedropper. Again, I fed the tan lizard. This seemed to placate it as it soon closed its eyes, then began to snore! I picked it up, lifting it onto my couch. Rolling my eyes, I grabbed a tea towel and covered it. "Night night," I whispered, pulling down my own double bed. Everything was jake until the early morning when I heard a series of whimpers.

"*What?!*"

I got up without wanting to, padding to the couch (a distance of some three feet) to check on the little troublemaker. It was shaking, its yellow eyes open and streaming . . . *tears?* Could lizards cry? Well, since this one was, I scooped it up and placed it gingerly beside me in bed. It relaxed, crawling onto my pillow to sleep on top of my *head*. I started to wonder if all that dough was worth it . . .

Every day, I had to take the cursed thing into the office. *What else could I do?* I'd played nursemaid enough in my life, had the maternal drive of Medea, and couldn't stand the sound of crying. Why Hughley picked me is a mystery for the ages.

A week passed. I was getting more used to the kid, who grew like a scaly weed. It was now about a foot tall—far too big for the "In" Box—and before long, sprouted up in jigs and jags until it resembled a toddler!

Maybe, I tried to rationalize, *things grow faster at the Earth's core.* I shrugged. My only concern was keeping it safe.

Until it switched on the radio. Rolling the chair from reception to just beneath a cabinet, it fumbled with the old Philco until it heard Jack Benny. Then, it clapped its claws, and . . . *actually laughed at the jokes!*

Something was as fishy as BirdsEye frozen cod!

"Uh, lizard," I said, mumbling. I felt like a fool. "Do you actually understand *that?*" I pointed up at the Philco.

It nodded enthusiastically, spreading those wings to float down beside me.

Now I was really sore.

What was Hughley's racket?

"Lizard," I said, "what gives? Where in Hades did you learn our lingo?"

It rolled its yellow eyes, crossing its claws.

"Hugh," it croaked, sounding hoarse. "He-he taught me."

Now I had to sit down. My eyesight had gone blooey.

"Did he now?" I asked skeptically. "Was that on your way up to the surface?"

The lizard nodded, small tan spines flopping over its neck.

"Yes," it squeaked. "After that, and in his office."

Even though I was in shock, I was still a sleuth.

"You mean . . . when you were an egg?"

It nodded again.

"Hugh taught me a lot. He tried to teach me planes, but that just made me snore."

I put a hand to my forehead. After helping to build them at Lockheed, I couldn't agree more.

"Okay, let's get some things straight. Are you a fella or a dame?"

It hmmped, flapping its wings.

"Fella, thank you so much!"

"Did Hughley give you a name?"

He put down his snout sadly.

"No."

"We'll get to that." I gave him the once-over. "What's with the wings? You some kind of flying reptile?"

Those yellow eyes went wide.

"You mean . . . you don't know?"

"I know Hughley was odd as hell. You some kind of rare species?"

That's when he grabbed his stomach, doubled over, and laughed.

"I'm warning you . . ." I growled.

"Look." He opened his mouth, revealing small, sharklike teeth, and took a deep breath. A small jet of flame whooshed out.

"Hey! You want to burn the joint down?!"

"Sorry," he said, hanging his head. "I just wanted to show you."

"Wise guy, huh? I'm no dumb Dora. Clearly, you're a dragon."

He clapped his claws together.

"Brava!"

"Why, you little . . . ."

I was stopped by a warning vision of dough flying out on wings.

"Hey, listen!"

He pointed up at the Philco, where a silky-voiced announcer intoned, "And now, Miss Eva Garden reads from Proust."

I started to open my mouth.

"Shhh!" he hissed. "She's one of my favorites!"

I slunk into my office, sitting and watching through glass as the dragon "oohed" and "aahed" at the actress' every word. She must have really liked Proust. I put my head on my desk and thought.

This creature had not only been taught by his finder, but, I surmised, from the radio, too. How else would he know Garden? And rush to turn it on? My brow hit a cracked leather pad. Was he some kind of cinemaddict?

Over the next fortnight, I found out just how much. When the blonde across the hall brought me movie magazines, the dragon nearly swooned. (I told her he was a fake, from Disney). He'd sit at reception for hours, eating up this slop like a starving man at The Big Boy. And he couldn't *stop talking* about all the stars he loved!

"It says here Little Annie is growing up! And she's playing a teenager!"

"Look at this shot of Ingrid Johansson! Her face is utterly flawless!"

"Did you know—?" He started up again.

"Look . . . dragon, I catch your drift. You love the movies."

"More than anything," he said, almost literal stars in his eyes. "Can we go see Errol Flynn in *Pirate's Penace?*" He sighed. "Now *that's* a real he-man!"

"I can get away with having you here," I said, "but not in a theatre. Sorry." He looked so small (though he was now seven-feet tall), I decided to throw him a bone. "Hey, I have an idea. Since you love Flynn so much, why don't we call you Errol?"

"'In like Flynn,'" he crowed, and I wondered if he knew what that really meant. Still, it didn't matter. I'd made him happy and that dough should fly my way soon.

This brought up another issue. Errol had an appetite as big as W.C. Fields' for booze. Every day for luncheon, I'd bring back burgers, hot dogs, fries, even fried chicken. He inhaled it like my Hoover. Now, I wouldn't have minded, except for one pesky thing: moolah. He was breaking my very low bank, making me do what I hated—asking Ma for a loan. But when he went through a pork crown, mashed potatoes, green beans, and a whole fruit pie every night, I wondered if I should go to Mass and pray hard for a client. It seemed Hughley, an oddball to the last, hadn't factored in Errol's expense. As far as Goldstein: he was shut tighter than Schwab's after midnight.

At the office, I engaged in productive work like doodling, while Errol listened to his favorite programs: Anything with Sinatra, *The Count of Monte Cristo*, and *The Adventures of Ellery Queen*. He was also partial to jazz and Benny Goodman.

I didn't mind. I *liked* Benny. But what began to bother me was Errol's liquid intake—going through bottles of Coca-Cola, A&W Root Beer, and even a glass of Bacardi every day! But since he was now so tall and more excitable than Lou Costello, I tried to cut down on his sugar. Even that didn't stop him from bouncing up and down when the blonde delivered his bounty.

Our forced camaraderie was ironic—like most things in L.A. Me, who'd lived my whole life in Hollywood, couldn't care less about the pictures. Meanwhile a newcomer, plucked from the earth's core, loved them more than anything! I tried to ignore his sighs as he listened to his sweethearts on the radio.

One afternoon, I sat with my head on the desk before I heard a scaly stir.

"Want another?" Errol asked, pointing to my bottle of Bacardi.

"No, thanks," I said, voice muffled by wood. Someday, I'd have to dust. "Right now, I'm more down than—"

"Bette Davis in *Now, Voyager?*"

"If you say so."

"What's wrong?"

"Well . . . my smacks are smacking me. As in, I'm nearly broke."

The fact I was consulting a dragon didn't say much for my sanity.

"Patience, sister," he said, swinging his spade tail. "If you keep me nicely, Goldstein pays you off."

I lifted my head.

"When?"

"He and Hughley didn't say."

"What do *you* know about dough?" I groaned.

He looked around my shoddy office, frowning.

"Well, *you* obviously need it. And your place ain't exactly fit for *Better Homes and Gardens*." Not even *Popular Mechanics*. "What you need is a client."

"And when one walks in, how do I explain *you*? Not everyone in this town is as dumb as Loretta."

I pointed across the hall.

"Hmm." Errol lifted a black talon to his chin. "Still, this *is* the land of make-believe."

"Uh—"

"The dream factory. Nothing's quite as it seems. So maybe you say . . . I'm prepping for a picture. I'm a serious actor and I like to get into the part."

"As-as a dragon?"

"Why not? Didn't *Oz* have flying monkeys? Am I really that off the wall?"

"Well . . . " I gulped. *I* was the one who was supposed to notice everything, but Errol had me licked. "All right. We'll give it a try." I wagged a finger. "But you *have* to stay in character whenever you go out."

"Deal," he said. "One more thing."

I groaned inwardly.

"I want to be your partner. All private dicks have them, according to Ellery Queen."

I gripped the side of my desk—the one that was noticeably sagging.

"You have *got* to be kidding!" I hissed. "You don't even have a license!"

"Oh." He looked crestfallen. "Well then . . . could I be your secretary?"

I jerked up like I'd been stabbed. I'd never been able to have one, and it *would* be nice . . . Then reality crashed through the room like a runaway Red Car. *"You're a dragon!"* I yelled.

"And a secretary. Even actors have to pay rent."

I swallowed. It was true: all over L.A., beautiful people came from everywhere to work as waiters, grease monkeys, shop girls—just a short stop before making it big.

"We'll try," I told him, "but if someone looks at you funny, this performance is over."

"Thanks," he said with a wide smile.

"All right. But put one claw out of place—"

"I'll be good," he promised, raising two talons like a Boy Scout.

"You'd better," I mumbled, "and no sneaking Coke! I'll know when your head hits the ceiling."

Dio mio! *I sounded just like Ma!*

I sat up in my chair as Errol happily loped to his now-official desk.

"By the way," he yelled back, "what's the pay in this joint?"

Chapter 9
Mrs. Felize Pays a Visit

My doodling was at a Van Gogh level when she first walked in. Her dark, curly hair wrenched into a stiff cascade perfectly complemented her decorous, below-the-knee skirt. She almost looked like a schoolgirl, but I, who had been one, knew better. This dame was no innocent, and I nodded at Errol to bring her in before he fell in love.

"Sorry about my secretary," I said, rising from my chair to greet her. "He's, uh, practicing for a role—in Mammoth Pictures' new fantasy."

The doll gave me a practiced smile, though her dark eyes reflected worry.

"Convincing," she said, standing before my desk.

"Please, take a seat." As she did, I caught the whiff of perfume wafting off her neck. Cheap. "How can I help you, Miss—?" I'd caught sight of her hand—no rock.

"Missus. Felize."

I nodded, trying to damp down my enthusiasm at having a real live client.

"My-my husband," she began, before bursting into tears. I passed her a hankie. In this racket, they came in handy.

"Affair?" I asked solicitously.

They had formed the bulk of my business before this drought which had settled on me like The Dust Bowl.

"N-no," she sobbed into white linen. "He's . . . he's dead."

Now *this* made me lean forward. Murder wasn't my usual beat.

"Can you tell me what happened?"

She blew her nose loudly, mascara streaking her otherwise pretty face.

"He-he was electrocuted."

I tried not to react, though I felt an inner chill. *The juice.* What a terrible way to go.

"And I take it you think he was murdered?"

Why else would she have come?

"I . . . yes. He's-he was a gaffer at Mammoth. It happened during a shoot."

"Cops on it?" I asked.

She shook her head.

"No. The-the studio wants to cover it up. Mr. Manly warned me."

I gave a wry smile.

"It won't be the first time." I thought back to Harlow's short-lived husband, another Joe "disappearing" from a yacht. Frankly, I thought Hollywood was all wet, but its scandals had even reached me. "So, I take it the coverup makes you suspect he was iced?" She nodded, sniffling. "I get twenty-five a day, plus expenses."

She opened her purse, handing over a wad of crushed bills. I fingered them. They seemed legit.

"Well, Mrs. Felize, don't worry. I'm sure I can crack this case." I shot her a cool glance. "So, why come to me? Why not Pinkerton or some man?"

"I-I thought a woman would understand."

Well, I thought, *murder crossed all genders.*

"Of course." I clucked my tongue in sympathy. "I'll get to the bottom of this. Start foxing around the studio. Can you tell me what film your husband worked on?"

"*Inferno Down Below,*" she said. "They were on Stage 27."

"Thanks."

"Thank *you*, Miss Forenza," she sniffed. She must have noticed my left hand too. As she rose, she handed me a note with her number. If I were a man, I suspected, she'd bat those dark lashes at me. I nodded, watching her swish her way out. She reminded me of a fancy coupe with a burbank top.

"Wow," said Errol, bending his way into my office. "Did you get a look at those gams?"

"Not interested. Have my own." He opened his mouth in a laugh, revealing teeth as sharp as he was. "Think we can trust her?"

"Sure." He nodded vigorously. "With pillows like that—"

"All men think with their short arm. Even a dragon. Frankly, I'm still on the fence. Something about that dollface doesn't sit right with me."

"*Let me come!*"

I blinked, bringing Errol into focus. He was jumping up and down.

"Huh?"

"To the studio! Oh please, I know all the stars—and I'd make a great sleuth. I just *know* it!"

I looked at his bouncing form. Most PI's *did* have a partner . . . and this one would work on the cheap. As far as muscle, well . . . he wasn't short in that department. And, like Matteo, if I called him my "apprentice," he wouldn't need a license.

"We'll have to get you a suit. Hollywood might be loose, but I still think they frown on nakedness. In public, at least. Outside the bedroom, you'd think they part of the Catholic League."

"Thank you, Nicky, thank you!" Yes, we were now on a first-name basis. "I swear—I won't let you down!"

"Better not."

I rose abruptly, causing my knees to creak.

Christ, at thirty-one, was I already old?

"Let's get cracking," I said. "It's off to Woolworth's for you."

Chapter 10
On the Case

We walked down to the dark, squat building at 6410 Hollywood Blvd., the huge letters in front spelling. "F.W. WOOLWORTH COMPANY." I knew the five-and-dime also sold clothes—since that's where I bought mine. Once we went through the door, I thought Errol might faint: The sight of the lunch counter, big enough to seat a platoon, brought a strangled gasp. I dragged him toward menswear, slapping his hand away from bulk candy in jars.

With a boldness I didn't feel, I approached the salesman.

"Good afternoon," I said, "my friend here needs threads. Preferably, a suit."

His nose shot up—far too far for Woolworth's.

"He appears to be a reptile."

"Well, you know in this town, appearances are deceiving. In fact, he's an actor."

"The studios," drawled the man, "have their own Wardrobe Departments."

"He doesn't need a costume," I said. "Errol here uses the Method—and he's *never* out of character."

"I see." This bird had all the warmth of a frosty Maine night in November. "Size?"

"Uh, not sure. It has to fit over his . . . scales."

"Indeed." He cast an appraising eye over Errol. "One moment."

The dragon turned to me.

"Is this going to work?" he asked nervously. "What if he throws us out?"

"Of Woolworth's?" I asked. "Hard to get much lower."

The haughty man returned, an enormous suit on a hangar drooping from his arms.

"This might do."

"Hey!" said Errol, "I may an actor, but I'm not Oliver Hardy!"

"We'll have to make holes for the wings," the salesman muttered.

And he did. After much faffing and sighing, Woolworth's finest made it work. Errol now stood before us in a brown three-piece suit, swatches of discarded fabric around him. The salesman added a matching tie which he of course had to tie. Then came a sharp brown fedora. But when it came to footwear, his magic seemed to fail.

"Um," he said, "I'm afraid we don't have quite your size. You might try Florsheim."

"That's Okay," I said. "How much do I owe you?"

The salesman took out a pad, adding up a row of numbers.

"That's thirty even." I gulped, withdrawing the bills. There went half of Felize's dough. "Please pay up front."

We did, and as we walked down the boulevard, Errol admired himself in every storefront window.

"Now don't get a swelled head," I told him.

"I can't. My hat wouldn't fit."

I laughed as we approached "Old Faithful," my fading '38 Ford. It would have been an embarrassment if it hadn't been paid for. As it was, it worked (usually), and that's all I needed. No gleaming Bentley for me.

I gestured for Errol to get in, and he did, slouching to save his head from hitting the roof.

"I just can't believe it!" he crowed. "Me, in a real-life jalopy! I've only seen pictures in magazines."

"Not like this one, I bet."

"Um . . . not exactly, but it's still a kick!"

"You keep that thought." Now came the hard part. I pulled up to the Mammoth gate on Overland, giving the old guard there my best smile. It mustn't have been too good, since once I cranked down the window, his hatted head was inches from mine. "I feel for you," I said, calling on the few mind tricks I'd picked up on the job. "I'm an ex-John myself."

His expression remained impassive: until he frowned.

"Who you here for?" He stared over at Errol but didn't react. Of course, he'd seen it all, from the Dracula to the Tin Man.

I fumbled in my bag. *Why did it have to be so big?* Whipping out my license, I hoped to impress.

"I'm a private detective," I said, "and I'm here to see Mr. Manly."

Despite his age, the guard straightened. He got that look in his eye like he'd just run into the Mob.

"Wait here." He stepped back into the open booth and picked up a black receiver. "Operator, it's the front gate. Could you connect me to Mr. Manly's office?"

I turned off the idling Ford. No one knew more about rationing juice than I did. I snuck a look at the guard. He didn't look too happy as he hung up abruptly.

"Mr. Manly's out of town," he said. *Sure . . . probably "fixing" a union strike.*

"Well, how 'bout his secretary? He explicitly called me in." Sometimes, in this racket, you had to tell a little white lie. I didn't like it, but I didn't like hoods either. I leaned out the window and whispered, "Some shenanigans on the set."

He gave me a knowing look. So, he'd heard about Felize.

"All right," he scrawled out a pass as I cranked up the engine. "But no snooping where your nose don't belong."

And with that, he waved us through.

I knew the seas would get rough once Errol entered the studio, but even I wasn't prepared for his open-mouthed awe. He was inside his own private fantasy: one with standing sets of New York and even a good-sized lake which boasted several old tubs.

As I parked where I shouldn't, gesturing him out of the Ford, my new partner could barely speak.

"Oh, oh my," he said, turning in a slow circle. "Oh, oh my."

"Snap out of it," I told him. "We have to get to the set. The one where Felize was killed."

Errol came down from his euphoria.

"And you think he was?"

"He was a gaffer—a guy who deals with lights. I looked it up when Felize left. Now, you'd think someone like that wouldn't get himself electrocuted." Errol nodded. "Follow me."

I'd never been here before but didn't want to look like a chump. I pretended I knew my way until we came to a structure labeled "27." It was rounded and huge, and I could feel a wind whipping between it and its fellow stages.

"Must be like New York," I said. I'd never been there, but all those tall buildings might create the same effect. Now, I strolled nonchalantly to the side of the stage, Errol in tow. We stopped before a light flashing redly from the wall.

"That means they're shooting," he whispered.

"Errol, I'm a PI. I managed to figure that out."

Once the light faded to white, I sidled next to a small door under it. It wasn't locked, which I found odd, but shrugged at luck's vagaries. I led Errol inside where we hung back in the shadows.

What a sight! Errol and I saw a reconstruction of Hell complete with billowing flames and even the smell of sulfur!

Mammoth, I thought, *got every detail right.*

Motioning to Errol not to move, I emerged from darkness to locate my prey: hopefully, a veteran union Joe.

I shortly found my man.

"Hello," I said in a low voice, just in case they started shooting. He was pulling some black, heavy cables and was dressed cooly in shirt-sleeves. He nodded between grunts. "Say," I went on, "you wouldn't happen to have known Larry Felize? Heard he was on this show."

The guy dropped his cables, his lined face looking older under a giant light.

"Yeah, I knew him," he said, looking down. "Can't believe it. But accidents happen."

"Yes," I purred. "And you're certain it *was* an accident?"

The guy looked startled.

"You mean . . . no." He scratched his scruffy gray head. "Still, Larry was an old pro. Been in pictchas since the Silents."

"Do you know if he had any enemies?"

"Well, not rightly. I worked on three other pictchas with Larry. He seemed a nice enough guy. Never gave the bosses no trouble."

"I assume when it came to electricity, he knew his onions?"

The guy nodded.

"Nobody better—not even Edison."

"Or Tesla," I muttered. "Were you on set when he died?"

"Yeah. It was yesterday. Larry and some other guys were setting lights for a shot. Larry was in the rafters—" He pointed to a high wooden scaffolding, "when—BOOM!—a huge key light fell right on his head. He didn't stand a chance."

"And he was electrocuted?" I asked.

"No ma'am. The weight of that light was enough."

A cold wave swept through me like the Bering Sea.

"Thank you," I tried to smile. "You've been very helpful." I picked up Errol, then dragged back to the Ford. "So," I told him, "seems sweet Mrs. Felize didn't tell the whole truth. Electricity played no part in her husband's death—sounds more like gravity."

"But why?" he asked, bending down to get in.

"That's what I'm wondering. "Time to give her a buzz."

Chapter 11
A Love Triangle—Or Not?

I had the operator try her line all day. That dame must have stepped out plenty since she didn't answer 'till night.

"Mrs. Felize, Nicky Forenza here."

"Yes?"

She didn't seem too glad to hear from me.

"Just checking on something. You said your husband was electrocuted. But I have it on good authority he was struck by a light."

"NOOO!" I heard, putting distance between myself and the receiver. That dame could sure squawk. "Mr.-Mr. Manly told me—"

"Say no more," I told her. "I'll be in touch."

Errol walked into my office.

"Well?"

"That Manly sure gets around. What do you know about him?"

"Hugh used to talk about him in his production meetings. The rumor is he's 'connected'—if you know what I mean."

"I'm Italian. What does he do at Mammoth—besides break kneecaps?"

"He's Meir Lenski's fixer: breaks up strikes, bribes the press—things like that. He's also a studio VP."

"What's he got on Lenski?"

"Knows all his secrets. Plus, he's a creep."

"With dangerous friends, I'll bet. What really gets me: Why would he put it around that Felize got juiced? Does he think it sounds more plausible?"

Errol shrugged.

"Hard to say. But being crushed by a light *does* sound suspicious. Who knows how these hoods think?"

"We need to," I mumbled. "Think like they do and nab 'em in the act."

Errol approached closer, looking all nerves, I thought. What was eating him?

"Why don't we grab some R&R?" he burst out.

"Huh?"

"Take in a flick. *Angels With and Without Wings* is playing at the Paramount."

I gave him a look.

"Nicky... please."

"Errol, we've been over all this. How do I explain a dragon in a suit? Especially to the ticket girl?"

"No Method?"

I shook my head.

"How 'bout... I'm doing a promo for my new Mammoth picture?"

"By sitting in the audience?"

"I'll hype the picture after our showing is over."

"I'm not sure."

"*Pul-lease?*"

He sounded like a bum pleading for half a buck. I sighed. How could I say no?

"All right. But try to keep a low profile."

This was hard when you had wings, but Errol did his best as we strolled down the boulevard. He looked so joyful I thought he might burst into song. I hoped not—I loathed musicals. I'd never in all my life met such a cinemaddict: not even Ma, still mourning over Valentino. As night descended, the Paramount, with its bright neon tubes and dotted-bulb foyer, was pretty darned hard to miss.

"Two please!" Errol chirped, walking up to the booth smack in the middle of the entrance. Of course, *I* handed over two bits, then went inside to wait in a short line for snacks. How could Errol watch his first movie without a tub of popcorn? Deciding to forego Cokes, I gestured for him to follow me over a lobby with carpet so plaid it actually made you dizzy. Once we arrived at the theatre proper, I whistled at the screen's floor-to-ceiling curtains, their top crowned by a design which looked like rolling hills. Naturally, Errol chose seats up front, and as I plopped next to him, I hoped I could see over several women's hats. In the meantime, my hand fought his claw for popcorn.

Why, I wondered helplessly, *had I even agreed to this scheme?* My deal was to care for Errol, not take him out on the town!

I brushed this aside as those gossamer curtains opened. The lights dimmed, and we were treated to coming attractions and Fox's Movietone News, which updated us on the war. Despite its upbeat tone, the footage made me jittery. With two brothers serving, the only real comfort I'd get was when they came home.

Once the titles rolled by, Errol, whom I feared would talk back to the screen, sat as silent as those fake sphinxes down the street at the Egyptian. He seemed mesmerized, absorbing through every scale this hokey tale of love and loss: two pals from the Bronx who served in the

Pacific—one made it and one didn't. The sound of sniffling rose as the young girl betrothed to the stiff pledged her love to his friend, which I found lousy but the audience ate it up. As a flurry of trumpets played "Taps" onscreen, the lights came up, and I snuck a look at Errol. He was sobbing into his popcorn, pausing only to whisper, "Why?"

Others were starting to look.

"Errol," I hissed, "it's all right. Just keep telling yourself, 'It's only a movie.'"

"I-I know," he sniffled, "but when Biff fell overboard—"

"I'm sure the actor is fine. He's probably home now counting his dough."

Though he nodded, wiping his eyes, I could see he was still blue.

"Hey," I said, "how 'bout we go out for a soda?"

"But-but what about the promo?" he said, lower snout trembling.

I waved a hand.

"Don't worry. This crowd is too shaken to notice."

We legged it down to Cherokee and Sontag's Drugstore, which I knew had a decent counter. After we'd snagged two sets, I ordered two large chocolate malts, heavy on the whip.

"So tonight, sugar's jake?" Errol asked.

"You've been through a lot. A whole war and the death of Biff."

He nodded, eyes still damp.

"I'm not sure I'll ever recover."

I raised a brow. *What*, I wondered, *made me get involved with this fruitcake?* Oh yeah, twenty-five G's. Still, Errol was so sweet in his movie madness that he managed to make me forget. The case. My screwy client. Visions of Pops freezing out in Montana. My thoughts were interrupted by the arrival of two glasses heavy with whipped cream, a single cherry perched on top. Even better, we received a small tin cup full to brimming with more malted! We both sipped greedily.

"Tell me, Errol," I said, my tongue loosened by ice cream. "What was it Hughley told you that made you such a film fan?"

I could almost see stars in his eyes.

"Well, he was a top producer. *Was*. He took over RKO to make his own pictures. Most featured Russ Jameson, the broad with the enormous—"

"—Rockets."

I nodded.

"Hugh mainly loved planes, but he loved movies, too. He wanted to be known as more than a pilot."

"Did any of his pictures make money?"

"You mean boffo B.O.?"

"Sure."

"*Scarface*. But *Hell's Angels* was a floperoo."

My straw made slurping noises as I got to the bottom of my glass.

"I guess you can't fault him for trying."

"I don't. A lot of fat heads think he was out to lunch, but to me he was killer diller."

I smiled.

Errol had clearly picked up from Hughley all the current slang.

"What say we take a powder?" I asked. "I'm not used to these late nights."

Errol consulted a large white clock face hanging behind the counter.

"It's nine-thirty," he said.

"Got to get that beauty sleep."

I handed over two bits before leading him back to the Proctor. I had to say I'd truly enjoyed this outing—maybe because I didn't have many friends. And Errol was on Cloud Nine.

His being a dragon didn't mean he couldn't have fun.

Chapter 12
The Commissary

The next morning, I woke to Errol's snoring. At least he was getting his Z's. As for me, I'd lain awake, trying to puzzle out why Felize had been bumped off.

Did he have a secret enemy—and was it his wife? If his death was really an "accident," why would Manly cover it up?

Something here stank, and it wasn't the L.A. River.

I jiggled Errol awake.

"No, no, Eva . . . !" he giggled, "we can't do that here!"

"Not even in your dreams."

I walked to the stainless percolator, pouring in some Folger's. Thank God the ration on coffee had ended last year.

Errol dragged off the couch, putting on his sleeveless, vest, and jacket. He struggled a bit to nudge his wings through the holes.

"Do I smell joe?" he yawned.

"Oh yes." I removed two chipped white mugs, filling them with the elixir. Without coffee, there would have been no PI's—and probably, no crime.

"Ahh," Errol downed his first cup, then walked two steps for another. I didn't take the papers—I could get them on the hoof—so when we were done, I set the two mugs down in my doll-sized sink.

"Where we off to?" he asked, straightening his hat.

"The office. I want to talk to that Felize dame."

We swung onto the boulevard in perfect weather: the sun regally graced us as white clouds glided by.

We had barely unlocked the glass door when the blower rang. I leant over reception.

"Nicky Forenza," I answered.

What came over the line was static and a frantic Mrs. Felize.

"Have you heard?" she cried. "A grip's been killed—Tony Alexander."

"How?" I asked, perching on Errol's desk.

"He-he was in the commissary," she said, "and went out when he was done. That's when someone shot him! But before they could see who, the gunman ran off. And Tony, he-he—"

Got iced, I filled in silently.

"All right, Mrs. Felize. Did you know this Tony?"

"Oh yes! I knew him from wrap parties. And he was . . . so young and handsome!"

I moved the receiver away from my ear. She was now sobbing. This was the part I wasn't good at: comfort.

"Now, now, Mrs. Felize. Just put your trust in me. This is valuable dope, and I'll get right on it.

Errol took the receiver from me and rested it in its cradle.

"Well?" he asked.

"Someone else's been popped."

Errol's yellow eyes widened.

"Who?"

"Guy named Alexander. Seems he worked with Felize."

Errol crossed his arms over his vest.

"Connection?" he asked.

I nodded. He'd be a good partner yet.

"Maybe."

"Back to Mammoth?"

"Yeah. Let's try to connect the dots."

This time, it was easy to get through the gate. Since the old guard knew me, he propped a pass on the inner windshield.. As we passed under the giant fancy letters which spelled out "Mammoth," I parked the Ford (illegally, of course) and consulted a studio map.

"This way," I told Errol, walking to Main Street to pass sets, stages, Props, and Panavision. How big was this damned place? It could house the U.S. Fleet!

I'd noticed a clutch of small trailers sprinkled outside the stages. Did these Hollywood types, I wondered, like camping on the lot?

I turned to Errol.

"What are they for?"

He puffed up his chest.

"Minor talent. Of course, the really big stars get their own private dressing rooms."

"Tough life," I commented, holding the door of the Commissary open. Once my eyes adjusted, I had to admit, I'd never seen anything like this: Men in chaps, holsters slung round their waists; next to Southern belles and a slick river gambler. I saw Indians (none of them real), Genghis Khan (*definitely* not real), and someone wearing a lizard head.

"At least you fit in," I whispered to Errol. He was so entranced I had to push him into the food line. When it was my turn, I ordered "MRS. LENSKI'S FAMOUS CHICKEN SOUP" for thirty-five cents. Errol, his appetite bigger, went for a burger and fries, a chocolate shake, and a Coke.

"What did I say about sugar?" I hissed, walking up to a table where an elegant man was seated.

"Do you mind?" I asked.

He gave a graceful half bow.

"Not at all."

Errol and I scrambled for chairs across from him.

"Hello," he nodded politely, cutting his lettuce leaves with a knife. A real gentleman!

"Good afternoon," I said, taking a spoonful of soup. *Dio mio, it was terrific!* "Do you work for Mammoth?"

He gave me a smile, revealing two rows of perfect teeth.

"Twenty-eight years and counting."

"Oh," I said. "And what do you do?"

"Sound mixing. Most thankless job on the lot: we're the last to finish a picture, and constantly yelled at to hurry."

Errol looked dreamy-eyed.

"They give Oscars for that, don't they?"

"Indeed," said the man. "I've got a couple myself." He chuckled. "They make a good doorstop."

I smiled. This guy liked to talk, and he'd been around. I eagerly held out my hand.

"Nicky Forenza," I said.

"Lorenzo Marconi." He leaned forward. "*Sei italiano, vero?*"

"*Si,*" I replied. *Con un nome come Forenza, è difficile negarlo.*"

He laughed.

"True, true. I've never seen you here. You a visitor?"

Before Errol could open his gob, I butted in.

"Yes, exactly! This place is so exciting!"

I stole a glance at a fake Indian. Not the stuff that dreams were made of.

Lorenzo nodded.

"For me, it's old hat. But I remember when I first got here . . ."

I decided to cut him off before he took that stroll down Memory Lane.

"I'm sure it was like a wonderland."

"IT IS!" insisted Errol.

"Uh, yes. Mr. Marconi, tell me, I've heard something dreadful from a friend who works in uh, Makeup." I leaned over the white oval table. "That . . . that someone was just shot here, right outside this building!"

Lorenzo's demeanor changed. He looked almost angry.

"Yes, that's true. Some grip was in an affair with a director's wife, and the director didn't like it. Shot the grip at point-blank range."

"And no one saw this?"

He chuckled.

"Of course, they did. There's always a crowd at lunchtime. But will they talk? Mr. Manly will see that they don't."

"Oh," I said, as if I'd never heard of the fixer. "That's horrible. My friend also told me that a gaffer was electrocuted."

I watched him carefully, but he didn't flinch at the lie.

"Word gets around," sighed Lorenzo. "Terrible mishap. But with so many men and so much equipment, sadly, accidents happen."

"I'd think," I said, trying not to sound too sharp, "this would apply more to stuntmen than veteran union crews."

"Well," he answered, shrugging. "We all live with danger."

"Is that so?" Was the mixer trying to tell me something? "Thanks, Mr. Marconi." I got up and nodded to Errol. "It's been charming to meet you. Perhaps we'll see you again."

He smiled at Errol.

"Maybe I'll mix your next picture."

Errol was so touched, he nearly burst into tears.

"Come along, uh, Ernie," I told him. "Back to the set with you!"

Errol opened his jaw to protest, then half-stumbled when he spotted one of his sweethearts.

"It's . . . it's Carole Lansing!" he breathed, stopping in front of her table where she huddled with other actors in makeup.

Expecting her to ignore him, I started when she threw him a wave and a kiss. Errol looked as happy as a starlet at her first screentest.

Maybe, I thought, heading for the door, *these Hollywood types aren't so bad after all . . .*

Chapter 13
Good Cop

When we got back to the office, Errol's claws seemed to float above the carpet. He took out his movie magazines, then spent the rest of the day mooning over Lansing. I let him be as I started pacing my office. It was so small I barely got in ten steps before I had to turn. Still, it was good for thinking.

What I knew so far ... Manly had lied to Felize's widow about the manner of his death. And what about Alexander? He'd been shot in full view of witnesses, but they'd clammed up like stiffs. They were afraid of Manly, and frankly, so was I. Errol had told me he was as good as a made man and had eaten a lot of pasta at the tables of the Five Families. He had an "in" with the Teamsters, and Errol said he wasn't a member but still got a generous pension. Not a guy you wanted to cross.

But was he involved in the killings? All I knew about gaffers and grips was what I read on the credits, and those were only names. Did they frequently end up dead? That's what I needed to know: not from the public record, since everything was hushed up, but from some insider who really knew the Business. Errol said that's what they called it: "Business" with a capital "B." Because in their minds, there was no other.

My heels had worn a pretty good groove in the carpet when I heard the front door open. Through the glass, I saw the welcome sight of Bill Anderson, probably the only LAPD cop not on the make. I smoothed down my hair, checking myself in my compact. It would do—at least for now.

"Hey, Nicky," he called, his brass buttons offsetting his blue uniform. Even now, I felt the tug of jealousy. The men got to be fitted out, while we women had to look like hospital orderlies.

"Bill," I smiled, trying to put the jumble of my current case aside.

"You eat?" he asked.

"Well, I had some very nice chicken soup, but I could use something else."

"Let's go to Schwab's," he said, taking my arm and nodding to Errol. "Great costume," he smiled.

As we took the stairs, I remembered the first time we'd met: He was stationed at City Hall downtown, while I, in my nurse's getup, was hidden away in the Woman's Bureau.

God forbid L.A.'s Finest should mix!

I'd first entered LAPD Headquarters to make a report, feeling much like a naughty intruder. Had it really been a year and a half ago? In those early days, Bill manned the front desk, as handsome as any movie star. His floppy blond hair and massive build almost made me forget the reason I was there.

"Hey!" he boomed in his big bass. "They let you out of the convent?" I blushed. Back then, I did that more often. "How can I do you?"

So many ways, I thought. What was wrong with me? *I was a nice Italian girl!*

"I, uh, need you to make a pickup at Union Station bus stop. There's a bird convinced he can fly, but I think he's just hopped up."

"Goofballs," Bill recorded, sucking on the tip of his pen.

How I wished I could be filled with ink!

"Description?"

Tall, blond, and handsome, I wanted to say.

"Uh, dark hair—like mine—" I played with a curl, "—badly dressed, trying to climb up a Greyhound so he can jump off."

"Shouldn't be too hard to spot."

Bill picked up a hand-held radio which came to life with a crackle. He called in my report, then gave me a big smile.

Damn, I thought. *Perfect lips!*

"So where've you been hiding?" he asked, leaning over the counter—so I could stare into those eyes. "Haven't seen you around."

"Like you said, I've been in the Order. They let us out to hear Mass."

He chuckled.

"Catholic?"

I winced. Would he drop me like a bad Communion wafer?

"Um . . . yeah. The worst kind—Italian."

His shoulders shook with laughter.

"Well, you do own the Pope."

"And you?" I asked, vaguely knowing the answer.

"Lutheran through and through. Nothing else for us Swedes."

"Oh. You're Swedish?"

I started to blanch, thinking what Ma and Pops would say.

"My grandmother was. I'm just a good ol' American."

"Me too. Though Ma still serves pasta for breakfast."

"And every Sunday, I get smorgasbord."

Come on, Nicky, I told myself, *enough with the small talk!* I wanted to know just one thing, but he got there a step ahead.

"So . . . married?" he asked, glancing down at my left hand.

"Nope," I said. "Ma says if I don't get hitched this year, it'll kill her." I waved a hand. "She's listened to too many operas."

He bellowed with laughter, holding his stomach.

"You're funny," he said, "and smart."

What about pretty? I wondered.

"I've always liked brunettes. My family is so pale, they could double as ghosts."

Now *I* laughed. There was nothing more attractive than a strong sense of humor! And all those muscles too . . .

"So," he said. "Tonight. You busy? I get off at five."

This put me into a tizzy: *Should I play hard to get? Pretend I had an engagement?*

"Sounds swell," I said instantly. "Should I meet you here?"

"Nah. I'll pick you up at the Sisters'."

For the rest of the day, my mind was *not* on paperwork. When Bill showed up at the Woman's Bureau at 5:05 on the dot, I wished I'd had time to change but there just wasn't time. So I threw a cheap jacket over my nursemaid's white, refusing to don a hat and gloves. Even though my beat was law and order, I would sometimes break the former and stick my tongue out at the latter.

Clustered around me, the other girls at their desks raised their brows almost in unison. They knew I didn't date much (to be honest, not at all), and the presence of this blond god set them all aflutter. As Bill took my arm, they each gave me the eye, as if to say: "Nicky, don't screw this up!"

I was determined not to.

Bill led me outside to a sleek Buick—I had a feeling he'd borrowed it. Once he'd helped me in, he started down Main Street.

"Where we headed?" I asked, just like Ma had taught me.

"Phillipe's," he said. "They invented the French dip."

"Good thing I like roast beef."

We arrived in just a few minutes. From what I'd heard, this place had been here since the Battle of Los Angeles: not the one a couple years ago, but a hundred. Kit Carson had been involved.

Once Bill came around to open my door, he escorted me into a room where most light was seemingly absent. Phillipe's was so dark you nearly needed a miner's cap, but Bill led me bravely to where we could order.

Of course, he paid—placing his coins in a small tray offered by the counter girl.

This place, I thought, *must really respect hygiene.*

We stumbled into an adjoining room, sitting down at an ancient booth. We proceeded to talk about everything: his parents, mine, our siblings, and the prospect of Japanese planes attacking L.A.

"I don't see it," he said, between bites of his dripping sandwich, washed down with a gulp of Coke.

"I don't know," I said. "What about Pearl Harbor?"

That infamous day came rushing back like a tsunami before it hits. Of course, it had been terrible: all those poor sailors killed. But, for me personally, the real horror was three months later.

"Angelo Forenza?"

When Pops answered the door, he didn't suspect a thing.

"Yes?"

I was standing behind him and saw a man in a charcoal suit flashing something shiny.

"May I come in?" asked the stranger.

"Sure, sure," said Pops, always friendly. His customers at the bodega loved him.

The man looked around, taking in our modest home: saw the portrait of Jesus, and Pops' hometown in Italy. He didn't seem impressed.

"You've heard of Pearl Harbor?" he asked.

"Who hasn't?" Ma asked from the kitchen. "Would you like a cappuccino?"

"No thanks," he said, taking a seat across from Pops. He wiggled as his backside hit a tear in the fabric. "I'm Frank Smith, FBI. You know we're moving the Japs into internment?"

"Yes," Pops answered, "but what about the Germans? Aren't they even worse?"

"Maybe," said Smith curtly. "That brings me to the Axis Powers."

"May the Pope curse them all tenfold!" Pops cried.

"Right. You understand, Mr. Forenza, that Italy is among them."

Pops snorted.

"That Mussolini! He should join the circus—maybe they need a new clown!"

"Earl Warren has provided my boss, Mr. Hoover, with a list of non-citizen Italians. Your name, Mr. Forenza, is on it."

"Well," Pops laughed, accepting a small cup from Ma, "I always meant to get naturalized—just didn't have the time. My wife here is American! Born in New York City."

"I see." Smith's face remained stony. "Are you familiar with EO 9066?" Pops shook his head, along with me and Ma. "President Roosevelt has asked for the relocation of certain enemy aliens living on our soil."

"What?!" Ma yelled, coming to hover over the G-man. "My husband is no enemy! He pays taxes, he gives out jobs! How can you call him an alien?"

"Sorry, ma'am," Smith said in a tone which showed he wasn't. He stood. "Mr. Forenza, come with me."

"But why?" Ma sobbed. "Where are you taking him?"

"Missoula, Montana," said Smith. "He'll be housed with other Italians."

"A prisoner, you mean! In his own country! How can you people do this?!"

"Just following orders, ma'am."

I couldn't stand it as Pops was fitted with handcuffs.

"Does it mean nothing to you," I shouted, "that I'm working on the P-38 at Lockheed? That we have a Victory Garden, and that my Pops gives every soldier store credit?"

"Afraid not. As I said, I have my orders." He looked over his shoulder as another man came to the doorstep. "Search everywhere," Smith told him. "You know what to look for."

He did. Within minutes, the agent emerged, hefting an old WW1 pistol, our shortwave radio, and even a clutch of flashlights.

I pointed at this last item.

"What?" I asked incredulously.

"They could be used to signal the enemy from the shore."

I laughed, almost hysterically.

"You think Mussolini's there, hiding in a sub?"

"It's no joke, Miss. This is wartime."

I was aware. We had blackout curtains and seldom drove. Ma hoarded ration coupons for sugar, coffee, and meat.

Smith faced me and Ma.

"The rest of this family needs to obey certain rules."

"Like what?" I nearly snarled.

"Until further notice, you're under curfew. You're not to leave the house from 8 PM to 6 AM the next morning. Any infraction can result in the seizure of your home or business."

"This isn't happening," I mumbled.

"Also, you'll need a permit to travel more than five miles from here."

"What about Lockheed?" I snarled. "It's in Burbank!"

"We'll make an exception."

"Swell. Thank J. Edgar for me."

"One more thing." I looked at Pops' face, scrunched up like a child's. He still hadn't fully grasped what was about to happen. "If I were you, I wouldn't be talking politics. At least, not out on the street."

"I have two boys in the Navy!" shouted Ma. "They're overseas right now, fighting for this country!"

"Commendable," said Smith, "but I don't make the rules. Let's go, Forenza."

One last frantic hug from me and Ma, and he marched Pops out to what I'd learn was "Fort Missoula."

"When will he be back?" I yelled. Ma was too busy sobbing.

"Unknown," Smith's pal said. "He's to be detained indefinitely."

My vision cleared. Here it was, a year later, after FDR had declared (on Columbus Day) we Italians were no longer enemies. So we could go out at night—maybe even own a flashlight. Didn't help Pops much though. He still froze in Montana along with Guiseppe and others.

Though he wrote when he could, Ma just wasn't the same. And my younger brothers were forced to work the bodega alone.

"Nicky?" Bill waved a hand in front of my face. *Some first date I was!* I tried to give him a smile.

"So, what do you like to do?" I asked. When you're not nabbing crooks."

"Oh, a few things. I like to bowl and go to the movies. You?"

"I'm not much for the pictures. But bowling is fun." I decided to get down to business.

"You, uh, you got a girl?"

"If I did, I wouldn't be here."

I blushed.

"Sure. Anything steady of late?"

A dreamboat like him must have to beat them off.

"Well," he sighed, "there was Lola."

Great. Sounded exotic.

"We called it quits last month. She wanted to settle down and I just wasn't ready."

I dipped my roast beef into gravy.

"I see."

"Hope that doesn't put a fly in the ointment."

I laughed.

"Not by a longshot! I didn't go to UCLA to get my 'Missus' degree."

He looked wistful.

"Wish I'd gone to college. But my pop couldn't afford it. He was a cop himself."

I nodded, giving him the once-over.

"How is it," I asked, "you weren't drafted?"

This was a man who could have taken France— himself.

"I was," he said, "but they need Johns on the force. Save everyone from you scheming Italians."

I flinched.

"I'm sorry," Bill said, reaching over to take my hand. "I hope I haven't offended you."

I shook my head. *How could he know?* Still, it took me a minute to recover. After that,

It was strictly small talk until Phillipe's closed, and I had gone home that night feeling like Catherine Medici. That had been the start and it only went up from there.

I jolted back to the present as Bill cruised down Sunset to Schwab's and its upscale lunch counter. Once we sat, I ordered a triple-decker—I was hungry!—and Bill grinned at the way I tore into it.

"Serves you right for trying to live on soup," he said, bumping my elbow. I noticed his uniform fit right in with the servicemen all around us.

"Hey," Bill gently nudged me. "You between Mars and Saturn?"

I laughed nervously.

"Guess so. Sorry. Got a lot on my mind."

"Wanna share?"

"You know I can't talk about cases."

In my game, this was a sacred rule.

"I'm a cop," he said. "You can trust me."

I laughed at the mischievous gleam in his eye.

"Well, as one ex-cop to another . . . no names, capiche?"

"Shoot," he instructed, digging into a thick slice of pie.

"Well, let's say there's this dame and her husband is dead. Now, she gives one version of how, but somebody else gives another. Then, a few days later, in the same, uh . . . office, another guy is whacked. This time, it's supposed to be a love triangle, but no one's seen a thing." I sighed. "Do you see any connection?"

"Not really, but *you're* the sleuth. I'd say it's awful suspicious those two deaths coming so close. *And* at the same joint."

I took a long sip of coffee. Black. Cream and sugar were for sissies.

"That's what I think," I said, "but I'm not sure how to prove it. Due to uh, circumstances, the second suspect is beyond my reach."

"And the dame—who I take is your client?"

"Right. I'm not sure about her. Might want to put on a tail." I thought. "What are you doing later?"

"Why, Miss Forenza," he put a hand over his badge-covered heart. "Are you asking me out on a date?"

Despite my feelings for him, I blushed.

"Well, yes, I suppose I am."

"Do you know where the missus lives?"

"I can find out. She gave me her digits."

"Good. Get me the address and we'll see how she spends her evenings."

"Thanks," I smiled. "Bill . . . I can't tell you how much I appreciate this."

"That's what friends are for," he said with a wink. "Though I wish—"

"Can we table that for now?" I flinched. "At least until after this case."

"Whatever the lady wants," he said with a half-bow. "Though *I've* been on a certain dame's tail for at least a year now."

"A year and a half," I answered. "I don't mean to lead you on. It's just with Pops a prisoner, Michael and Tony away, and me trying to breathe life into my business—"

"While training a new assistant?"

"Oh, Errol." I waved dismissively. "Never hire an actor."

"Unless it's to stare in a mirror."

We both laughed, and I felt easier. With Bill at my side, I could see myself catching the killer.

Chapter 14
The Women

Once I got back to the office, I pulled out a lumpy White Pages. There she was, Kim Felize, right alongside her husband Larry. The phone number matched. I called Bill, giving him the Valley address. Then, I waited, watching Errol through the glass door. He was in mid-program, swooning over some knockout: one he could only hear. An hour later, the ameche rang and I picked up.

"Forenza," I said brusquely.

"Nicky." I heard Bill's comforting bass crackling from a payphone. "Felize doesn't believe in drapes."

"Figures," I snorted. "Giving the neighbors a show."

"I can see her getting ready, and boy, is she glamming it up. If our date's still a go, better slip on your best dress. How soon can you meet me?"

"I don't think the old Ford can make it to the Valley."

I'd only gone there for Lockheed—and that was on the streetcar. Now, I tried to avoid it.

"Look," Bill said, "I'll tail her to wherever she's going, then swing by to pick you up."

"Good. I'll bet she's headed for town."

I hung up. Now, my only worry was finding a suitable dress. I knew there were none in my closet (more like a cubbyhole) where my work skirts and blouses lived. No, tonight I'd need something special: like those getups the movie stars wore. And just a few steps away, I had an in-house expert.

"Errol," I called, "how'd you like to help me go shopping?"

"*Yah!*" he cried, even ignoring the Philco. He started to bounce. "Back to Woolworth's?"

"Not this time. I need to look like Eva Lansing."

"Carole."

I nodded, finding the Ford on a curb. Errol dodged traffic as he bent his way in.

"So where to?" he asked eagerly. "Is this for a date with Bill?"

"Well . . . kind of," I admitted.

"Then there's only one place—Adrian's! That's where the stars get their gowns."

I frowned.

"Where's she at?"

"*He!* And his shop's in Beverly Hills. I *think* on Beverly Drive."

"That Beverly sure got around."

I took Sunset past the Mocambo with a line of autos out front. After that was the Little Troc on the Strip, its bland exterior hiding what I guessed was glamor within. I also knew that on Sunset, behind tall foliage and gates, there were some serious houses. *Mansions,* in fact, ornate enough to entertain royalty while shielding their facades from our unworthy eyes.

"Jeepers," said Errol, mouth agape. I just hoped he didn't drool over the stick. I slammed one heel on the clutch, switching into low gear. Even in late afternoon, the Strip was jammed. When the Ford made a scary sound, I prayed we could reach Beverly before she left for the day.

A quick turn on her drive, with its swanky shops and even swankier women, then a couple blocks down to a white, rectangular building. Strange thought, but it resembled a mausoleum. Once Errol leapt out with a squeal, I followed slowly behind, seeing through the now-open door a sterile white space where a motionless model sprawled.

"Is she dead?" I whispered to Errol.

He laughed, then turned to greet a shopgirl so glamorous she could have been on the screen. He bowed, then bent to kiss her hand. The young woman tittered.

"What picture are you on?" she asked.

He opened his mouth to stammer, but I quickly cut in.

"Journey to the Center of the Earth."

"Ooh," she cooed. "I'll be sure to see that one. When's it coming out?"

"Next year," I said smoothly. "Lots and lots of effects."

"I see." She gave me the once-over and if her nose had gone any higher, it would have burst through the roof. "How can Adrian's help you today?"

Now it was Errol's turn.

"You know that off-the-shoulder pale blue Renata Heywood wore in *Cover Girl?*"

"Sure," said the shopgirl. "Who doesn't?"

"Me," I answered, "and I'd like something modest. Nothing frontless or backless."

Errol sighed.

"How about that gold halter number Carrie Joanford wore in *The Women?*"

The shopgirl thought—it seemed an effort.

"Well, that was an Adrian. But it's somewhat out of fashion. Let me see if there's a copy in the back."

As she swayed past, I caught a swirl of perfume. Delightful. When you worked in Beverly Hills, you better wear the best. I turned toward Errol, finding myself nearly blinded by all that white. And high above our heads: was that an actual *dome?*

"Halter?" I asked him suspiciously.

"No need to stew. There's so little flesh exposed."

"Fl-flesh," I stuttered, but was halted by the shopgirl who clutched a beaded gold frock. "This way, please, Miss—?"

"Forenza," I mumbled, hoping she wouldn't mistake me for the enemy.

But the delicate blond seemed unmoved. With a crooked finger, she led me into a dressing room—as big as my apartment. She stared at me quizzically.

"Aren't you going to get undressed?"

"Uh, yes, I mean no . . . do you think you could leave?"

Her mouth curved into a smirk.

"I'll be right out here if you need me."

Mother Mary, how did you put this thing on? There was a lower layer of draped fabric, then a shimmering gown with wide straps and a cutout below the breasts! The bra was attached to the waistband by a single jeweled strand. I groaned into the mirror, looking like a girl held in a harem. *Please God,* I thought, *may Ma never see this!*

What if I trip? I wondered. *Or bend down too far?* Once I'd wrestled with straps to get the darn thing on, Errol burst through the dressing room door!

"Va-va-voom!" he whistled. "You outdo Harlow in *Platinum Blonde!*"

The blonde before us put her hands on her hips.

"I must say, I'm gobsmacked," she said. *Who'd died and made her British?* "It just needs to be taken out a bit in the hips . . . and lengthened about three inches . . ."

She clapped, and a seamstress appeared as if summoned by magic lamp. The older, dark-suited woman stuck some pins in her mouth and knelt. If I were being honest, I didn't hate the dress—in fact, it looked pretty good, but one looming question threatened to bring down that dome.

"How much?" I asked.

"Twelve hundred," said the seamstress. "And you'll need a fur to go with it."

I jerked so violently she almost swallowed a pin.

"*What?*" I yelled. "I've never paid more than twenty!"

"She's talking 'thousands,'" Errol smiled, giving me a reptilian wink. He turned to address the salesgirl. "Did I mention Miss Forenza worked closely with Mr. Hughley?"

"The off-the beam-billionaire?"

"Exactly," said Errol. "Although he's tragically left us, he did will my partner here a substantial stack of clams."

The shopgirl's too-thin frame froze.

"Well, in *that* case," she said airily, "we'll put it on a bill. Plus a floor-length mink and of course matching shoes."

"Of course," I nodded, trying to pull those harem pants up.

"We can't forget makeup!" said Errol. "And could we please shake a leg? My partner has an evening engagement."

"Yes, *sir!*" snapped the seamstress with everything but a salute. A multitude of pins and a few stitches later, I was encased in the gown:

as in, to take it off, I'd have to use scissors. Then I was ushered to the shoe section for a pair of strappy, gold, heels—at least five inches tall. After that came the tasteful gold handbag, into which you could fit maybe a lipstick. Blondie grabbed my arm and hurried me to the back which looked like the Beverly Wilshire. Another young woman—this one brunette—applied make-up as I stood, since I didn't think I could sit. I was handed a small mirror. Not bad. *Eat your heart out, Carrie Joanford!*

"You could be in *Photoplay!*" breathed Errol, throwing a white mink around my shoulders. He bowed and led me out. "After you, Duchess," he beamed. Before the door closed, he shouted back, "Tell Adrian thanks!"

Chapter 15
Mrs. Felize Steps Out

It was hard to drive in a dress so tight it squeaked, but I made it back to the office. Once Errol and I stepped out of the elevator, I heard a horn buzzing down the hall. Fumbling with my keys, I stumbled in and seized the receiver.

"What?" I yelled into it.

"Nicky, where you been? I've been calling and calling."

"Sorry, Bill, but I'm back now."

"That's good, 'cause I'm right outside."

I heard him click off the payphone.

With difficulty, I tottered on those heels down to the old elevator. I seemed overdressed for this joint, proven by Bill, who just stood there, handsome as anything in a fitted dark suit.

"Nicky?" he asked, unsure.

"Uh, hi, Bill," I smiled, blushing. What was wrong with me? Did Sam Spade ever blush? I wrapped that gorgeous mink tighter around my shoulders as I accepted his hand. Even though *I* was the one in the heels, he stumbled on the way out. "Careful, now," I told him. "If you can't handle an inch, how would you fare with five?"

"I hope," he said, escorting me out, "to be able to answer that some day."

"*Bill!*" I admonished, swiping him with my gold bag. It didn't do too much damage. "What's this?" I asked, eyeballing a sleek convertible coupe that must have been brand new.

"A loan," he grinned, helping me inside. "Sometimes, the Chief comes through."

"Why not?" I shrugged. "It's not like his money is clean."

Once we got going, I leaned back to enjoy the breeze of a balmy November night. Yes, it was still hot: "swimming weather," as they say. The mink was completely superfluous, but somehow, I didn't mind. It was fun to get all dolled up—*occasionally.* If I had to do it each day, I'd beg for the men in white coats. My hair blowing, I turned to Bill, who clearly enjoyed driving something not black-and-white. "Where are we headed?"

"Ciro's," he said with a smile.

"Wow. For a gaffer's widow, Mrs. Felize lives high on the hog. Ever been there?"

He snorted.

"I'm lucky if I can afford the counter at Thrifty's!"

"I'm right there with you," I said. "When I first started my business, even *that* looked steep. A nickel for a cup of joe? C'mon!"

We both laughed easily as we cruised down Hollywood Boulevard, turning on Laurel to head south down to Sunset. Second time today for me. Usually, I didn't go out at night unless I was on the job, and then I was busy hiding. But now I saw the boulevards blazed in neon, from the Chinese to the Egyptian; from Schwab's to Alpha Beta. The bright theatre marquees lit up billboards asking us to buy war bonds.

My world, usually black and white, erupted into colors worthy of a Mammoth road show.

Before long, we were there, on the Strip in front of Ciro's. It didn't look like much—just a plain building with the name in neon. As Bill stopped, an eager valet ran toward us and, after taking over, parked the coupe beside a couple of Rolls. Once the doorman let us in, I felt like I'd been lifted from Hollywood to uh . . . Hollywood. We saw a fake wood "scroll" hanging by the entrance, and even *I* knew these names: Mary Pickford, Bob Hope, Roy Rogers, Lucille Ball. I felt I'd been granted an audience in a kind of heavenly throne room. *And the décor!* Overhung with drapes, a pure white piano beckoned from the bandstand, while tasteful plants crawled from floor to ceiling over white-clothed tables. Still, the people there added the best and final flourish: Movie royalty who deigned to live among us; famous, flawless faces; the women perfectly made up and coiffed, casually lounging in backless gowns next to dark-suited dates.

Bill murmured something to the Maître d' as I halfheartedly gave my mink to the coat check-in girl. Even *she* was gorgeous. Bill must have slipped Frenchie some dough since we were immediately seated just off the crowded dance floor—and directly *across* from our quarry. I forced myself not to look at spinning dancers but at a transformed Mrs. Felize.

She'd gone from the mouse in my office to a tigress on the prowl. But what really caught my interest was her dinner companion: suave, tall, and wearing a white tux, of all things; he stood out like a nebula amongst this cluster of stars.

I leaned over the pristine white tablecloth, set with more silverware than I'd ever seen in my life. What was with the three forks?

"Who is he?" I whispered across to Bill.

But he didn't hear. He was taking me in sans mink, the glitter of gold beading reflected in his blue eyes. When he looked below my breasts, he saw a flash of flesh. *Oh, brother! What had Errol gotten me into?*

"Wow," he breathed, taking my hand across the table. "Nicky . . . you're an absolute knockout. Where've you been hiding all this?"

"In a closet I can't afford?" I quipped.

Damn! I'd done it again! A blush spread from my face to my collarbones.

"What I mean," Bill went on, "is if I knew you cleaned up like this, I'd have taken you to every damn swanky joint in town!" He looked cowed. "I'm sorry. I shouldn't curse in front of a lady."

What lady? I looked around, realizing he meant me! It was sometimes hard to remember when I was hiding behind some palm, snapping away at a cheating spouse. Hey, that reminded me . . .

"Who's with Felize?" I stage-whispered. "Some Hollywood type?"

"Yeah. I did some research. When he picked up the grieving widow, I took out the old Kodak. Had the pics developed downtown, then showed 'em around. Phyllis in Dispatch practically swooned: says he Don Lockwood, some juvenile lead at Mammoth." He smirked. "Looks like a man to me."

I nodded. If Lockwood was a juvenile, then I was still in grade school.

"So Felize is making Lockwood," I said. "Wonder if old Larry knew." I rose unsteadily, heels slipping on carpet. Restraining an unladylike curse, I threw back my shoulders and approached the happy couple. Just like Carrie Joanford. "Mrs. Felize," I said, not bothering to fake a smile, "what a coincidence! I didn't know a gaffer's wife could afford a joint like Ciro's." I winked at Lockwood. "Or perhaps your friend is paying."

"Nicky Forenza," Felize hissed, her breasts so exposed I could swear they winked at me. "I wish I'd never met you!"

"Then why did you? Why seek me out when you're not exactly in mourning?"

"I needed a credible witness. Someone to say Larry had been juiced."

My mind whirled faster than those dancing couples.

"Insurance money. I see. And Manly was going to help you?"

Her dark eyes glazed.

"Not exactly. I thought—"

"If you covered up the *real cause*, the insurance would cough it up quicker. How much?"

"Five grand," she spat.

"And I take it your dead spouse didn't know about Mr. Lockwood?"

He stiffened in his chair, turning toward his date.

"Hey—who is this broad, anyway?"

"A private dick," Felize growled. "One who I thought could help me. Instead, she wants to put me in the cooler."

"Don't mistake me, Mrs. Felize." I shook my hips to blind her with gold. "I don't give a hoot about you. Or even your five-grand scam. But I want to find out what you hired me for: Who killed your husband?"

"Like I know!" she said a little too loudly. Beautiful faces turned. "Maybe it *was* an accident." She gave me a cold smile. "But a happy one."

I winced.

"One more thing.," I said. "What about Tony? You said he worked with your husband."

She twisted her mouth, a red smear of lipstick.

"Yeah, and that's *all* I know. Why don't you get back to your man? He looks a little edgy. In other words—shove off, sister."

I raised an etched brow.

"Until we meet again."

"Well?" Bill asked, all nerves, after I'd resumed my seat.

"Call it spooky or woman's intuition, but I don't think she killed Felize. Or even had him killed," He nodded, handing over a crystal glass half-filled with white wine. I took a big sip. Delicious. "Honestly, she's just your neighborhood floozy who took advantage of fate. And I don't think she's got the smarts to pull off a hit. Besides," I added, "she doesn't have the C-notes to pay for it."

"Yeah," Bill agreed, staring down at the menu. "Well, we might as well order. I'm already set on the veal scallopini."

"Why, Officer Anderson!" I fluttered a hand to my neck. "Have you gone crooked too?"

He winked.

"Not a chance. But I've been saving my meager wages for a night like this. And I intend to eat like a movie star—and dance like one, too!"

After I gorged on lobster newburg, chased down by a crab leg on ice, we joined those gyrating couples, and for the first time ever, I swayed in a conga line! It was fun, it was wild, and I loved every second: despite my client glowering from her table. I hoped I hadn't ruined her date, but, feeling Bill's hands on my shoulders, I knew I was loving mine!

Chapter 16
Number Three

When Bill took me home, the coupe flew past the now-dimmed lights of Hollywood. Wartime blackout rules. As my hair blew back, I felt so much lighter than I had in awhile. I'd eliminated—*maybe*—one suspect from the case—but didn't have another. I shook my head.

C'mon, Nicky, I told myself. *Concentrate on the guy throwing you white-hot glances.*

He parked in front of the Proctor, walking round to open my door. After I stepped out, I was on the verge of stifling propriety by asking him to come up. Alas, before this crime could occur, he walked me into the lobby, kissed me on the cheek, then mumbled, "Goodnight, Nicky" before swinging out the front door.

Darn! Why did he have to be such a gentleman? Why couldn't he sweep me into his arms, bend me back, and whisper, "I want you," before carrying me up the stairs, Rhett-and-Scarlett style?

Was I not attractive enough? I wondered, punching the elevator button, *to stir something in him?* I knew something sure stirred in me!

Granted, I hadn't gone "all the way" with my college boyfriend, a nice Italian boy whom Ma and Pops had loved; but now, with Bill, whose blond head and WASP moorings sent Ma into conniptions, I wanted to know what I was missing.

Not very "ladylike," but who said I was a lady? Oh yeah. Bill.

When I twisted my studio's doorknob, I realized it wasn't locked, and out of that Adrian bag I pulled a crammed-in .38. In this outfit—draped in white mink, with patches of flesh peeking out—I wasn't exactly a Marlowe who could cow an intruder—but I gave it my best shot, using my heel to kick open the door before shouting, "FREEZE!"

"Calm down, partner," Errol drawled from the folds of my couch. He looked comfortable enough as he put aside a *Photoplay*.

I lowered my heat.

"How'd you get in here?" I asked. If Bill had fulfilled my wishes, Errol would have been a very awkward third wheel.

"Girl downstairs is a sucker for good-looking men."

"More like a nice suit," I cracked. "And I'll be talking to her. What are you doing here?"

"Even a dragon," he said, "deserves a pillow and blankie."

"You're right." I threw those items at him, then rummaged in a drawer. "Here's my extra key."

"So, did you find that floozy?"

"Yup. Turns out her racket is fraud. To the tune of five G's."

"From Manly?"

"Insurance. And speaking of which, we need to track Tommy down."

He started.

"This is a gag, right?"

"Nope. I'm as serious as you are about Carole Lansing. Everything on this case seems to lead back to him."

"But—you know who he is?"

"You told me. Hughley thought he was part of the Mob."

Errol looked scared. I threw off the mink, half-glad to be rid of its weight.

If a billionaire *steered clear of Manly*, I thought, *how could I get him to talk?*

"We have to be careful," I said. "Find out where Manly is now and keep a tail."

"What'll that tell us, besides he's a capo?"

"Or capo dei capi." Errol looked puzzled. "Boss of bosses. Better brush up your Italian."

"I think we should wait to confront him 'till he's back in town." I was about to object. "Look—he's having crew guys bumped off. So far, only at Mammoth. If we tail him there, we might bust up a meeting. Between him and his consiglieres."

I laughed.

"I don't think his trouble boys dare to give him advice. Still, your plan is sound." Errol puffed out his chest. "We'll start tomorrow. Try to find out his schedule. For now, I'm beat. Let's you and I get some shut-eye."

The next day, I managed to coax the old Ford to the Overland gate. I peered out at the guard. Darn. My friend wasn't on duty, and this called for some charm.

"Good morning!" I chirped like a wide-eyed ingenue. "I'm here to see Mr. Lenski. Tell him it's Nicky Forenza and I'm a private detective. He'll know what it's about."

The guard, young and weary, with partially grown-out hair telling me that he'd been discharged, reached for the phone in his booth. Frowning, he barked into it, then handed me the receiver.

"Mrs. Forenza?" asked a female voice. "Mr. Lenski is out. He's at the Hillcrest Country Club."

"That's fine. Actually, I wanted to speak to you." An old shamus trick: Always be nice to those on the bottom. Someday, they'd be at the top. "Do you by chance know when Mr. Manly will return?"

I heard the shuffle of papers.

"Um . . . oh yes. He'll be back on the lot this afternoon."

I felt a tingle like when I looked at Bill.

"Thanks so much," I said. "I'll commend you to Mr. Lenski."

"Swell!"

Once the phone clicked off, I returned it to the ex-GI.

"We'll be back in a jif," I said. "Mr. Lenski's office will clear us."

"Sure."

He didn't look too convinced as he waved for me to make a U-turn.

Once we were outside the gate, Errol, slumped as always, turned to me.

"Where to now?" he asked.

I heard my stomach growling.

"How 'bout Pink's?" I'm jonesing for a chili dog."

"Yum!" said Errol, eyes shining. "What are we waiting for?"

I left Overland, taking Washington to Pico, then made a left on La Brea. *There it was!* The hot dog stand that had stood in for friends when I was feeling down. Now, since it wasn't lunchtime, there wasn't the usual line. **"Hot Dogs," "Tamales"** blared at me from an awning. I parked the Ford, ordered, and handed over two bits (including a nickel tip). My reward was two plump dogs smothered in tasty chili. Errol and I walked to the art deco filling station next door, both leaning against a white column as we munched away. The joy of Pink's was almost celestial. Even though it was fairly new, word spread across L.A. A fact Errol swallowed along with three other dogs.

"No Coke?" he asked sadly.

"Okay, just for now. That chili is pretty blazing." Satisfied, we walked it off by heading east down Melrose. When we came to Gower, I saw a sign, "Hughley Studios." I turned to Errol. "So that's where the sap sunk most of his dough."

"Naw," said Errol. "To him, these were coins you find in the couch."

"Still," I sighed, "all those billions and he gets himself killed in a plane crash. Too bad he didn't stay home."

Errol nodded, looking down.

"I miss him," he said.

"I guess, in a way, he was your . . . pop."

"Yeah. I never knew my real one."

I patted his claw, then stepped back, filled with a kind of strange horror.

"Don't tell me," I yelled, *"that that makes me your ma!"*

We exchanged a somber glance, then started to laugh.

"More like a sister," said Errol. "And always . . . a partner."

"Let's go before I have to get out my hanky."

We walked a good half-hour to get back to the Ford and Pink's. Before climbing in, I gave the guy manning the stand a salute.

Since it was now past luncheon, traffic wasn't too bad, and the face of that guard appeared before I realized we were back at Mammoth.

"Mr. Lenski—" I started.

"Okay, sister, you're jake."

From his hand, I grabbed a small paper pass and perched it against the windshield. This time, I drove across Main Street to Thalberg, snagging a rare "Visitor" spot.

"Parking magic," I told Errol, getting out. He straightened as he did the same.

We hoofed it to head honchos' building, its stately white columns somber. If you didn't know better, you would have thought Thalberg had served on the Supreme Court. Inside, we went through the usual dance: first-floor receptionist, elevator, guard swinging his keys so we could enter the Hallowed Nave. But this time, we didn't make for the corner office, heading instead to a nearby wood door marked "Mr. Manly." Now all we had to do was wait for the hood to appear.

I loitered by the brass water cooler as Errol pretended to look out a window. From his expression, I could tell he was walking on air at the thought of the giants who'd worked here. *My* thoughts, though, tended more to indigestion. *Damned chili dogs!*

Finally, we heard that door creak open. Two guys walked out and if they weren't Cosa Nostra, my Pops wasn't from Italy. I gave them the eye, then decided to be cute.

"Ciao, come stai?" I asked with a smile. They exchanged a dark look before slumping toward the elevator.

The heavy door opened again. A dark-complexioned man in what looked like a Saville Row suit stomped down the hall. Manly. Guess he didn't want to be seen with his boys.

I nodded to Errol, and we followed—casually—only we took the stairs.

Where the hell was Manly headed? He trailed his goons by a sound stage's worth of space, hands in pockets, back slightly bent. Even from behind, you could tell he was trouble. We tailed him as he passed what must have been admin buildings: this part of the lot was dull—not a standing set in sight! At last, the two goons stopped before a high white sound stage, the breeze stirred between it and its neighbors whirling against my ears.

Manly nodded, jingling a set of heavy keys before unlocking a nondescript door. He and his men stepped inside, tailed (not too closely) by a determined dame and a dragon. We slunk through the door quietly, and, standing back, I surveyed the scene. Based on the huge piles of lumber and no constructed sets, this stage was not being used. It was dark, which was good for me and Errol.

"No one to bump off here," he whispered.

I nodded.

"Listen." I heard a rough bass. Manly. "I don't like all this publicity. Can't you pay off the bulls like always?"

"Sure, Tommy," said one of his boys. He sounded sorry—and scared. "It's just that . . . two hits in the same week? It don't look good. We're trying to dummy it up, but you know studio folk—they eat up rumors."

"All rumors are true," Manly growled. "That's why we gotta stop these. Did you put the squeeze on those gossip dames?"

"Yes, sir," said another voice. Older. "They won't squeal. They know what happens to them that does."

"Good. Now, I want you here every day. Keep your peepers open. Anything screwy goes down, you tell me quick. Mr. Lenski don't like it when his employees are blipped—he prefers to think they're part of the 'Big Mammoth Family.'"

He spat.

"Sure, boss."

I elbowed Errol and we beat it, squeezing through the small door. We walked briskly back to the Ford, hoping not to be spied by Manly.

After two tries, the engine turned over. This time, I went out the other gate, hightailing it up to Washington. Errol, though scrunched, was curious.

"What the dickens was that all about?" he asked.

I tried to make sense of it all.

"Basically, we've confirmed what we knew—Manly is Lenski's fixer. And he'll do *anything* to duck bad PR. Question is: Does that include murder?"

"I don't think so," said Errol. "He never mentioned Felize or Alexander; didn't give orders to blip anyone else."

"He's cagey," I said. "Leaving his office. Probably thinks it's tapped." A yellow light turned to red, and I pressed the clutch, downshifting into neutral. "Maybe . . . " I thought. "Maybe those hoods used some code we didn't get."

Errol shook his head.

"That 'chat' was pretty straightforward."

My frown was deeper Manly's. *Something* was going on—two stiffs attested to that. But did Manly order the hits? And why go after the little guys, so far down the union pole they rarely flashed by in credits? I was also all nerves due to something else. Now that Felize had her dough (and hated me), she was no longer a client. That meant an end to her meager payments. Which left me with exactly *niente.* Bupkis.

But could I in good conscience abandon a case already strewn with bodies?

"Errol," I told him, "we've got to tighten our belts. For you, that means twelve notches."

He looked terrified. But what else could I do? Then a plan filled my head, ringing with the force of the Queen of Angel's bells. Time to see the big man himself.

Chapter 17
The Lion Roars

With Manly likely prowling the studio, I decided to give it a day. I parked the Ford (illegally), and when Errol and I went back to my joint, he brewed me a cup of joe. Once he'd sprawled on the couch, I paced around him. Since the space was so small, I passed him every ten seconds.

"This is screwy," I mumbled, sipping from my mug reading "Proctor Hotel" in faded letters. The only thing the landlord had ever given for free.

I slumped into a chair.

"We need to pray." I said, "Lenski will shell out for catching this killer."

"Or killers," Errol added.

"Hmm. I guess that's right." I took another sip. "I wonder if Manly knows Frau Felize. Would he have paid her to off her husband?"

"You said you thought she was clean. And how would she mingle with Manly? He's so far above her he's in Hoodlum Heaven."

"Yeah." I sighed. This was getting me nowhere. "What about motive?" I asked. "Mrs. Felize was after five G's, but Manly? Why would he mess with a gaffer?"

"Was he not being lit on his good side?"

I chuckled.

"Let's put this to bed. Tomorrow, it's back to Thalberg."

"Tell him it's *important*. Tell him it involves Mammoth's two murders."

The plump, elderly secretary, whom Errol told me was called "Scheherazade" since she had to read scripts aloud for the non-reader Lenski, started from behind her desk. She must wonder how I got in here, but that was between me and the front gate.

"Very well. Wait here," said this spinner of tales, opening one of two wooden doors to consult with her boss. She emerged surprisingly soon, but her face was grim. "Mr. Lenski will see you," she snapped with the warmth of a mortician. "You have five minutes."

"Two-and-a half for each murder?"

The woman huffed.

"There has not, and never will be, a murder on this lot."

"So many 'accidents,' though?"

Errol stayed behind as I entered the inner sanctum. The double doors behind me shut on their own. *Movie magic?* I looked up. There, across a space as big as Buckingham Palace, sat a middle-aged man, nattily dressed, with round owllike glasses. What little hair he had was thinning and white.

"Mr. Lenski," I said, sprinting a fifty-yard dash to get to him.

"And you're the lady dick?" He assessed me from head to toe. "Not bad."

I nodded.

"Back at you. Mr. Lenski, I'm sure you're aware that within a few days, two people have died here at Mammoth."

"Oy!" he exclaimed, running a hand over his pate. "Just my luck! It couldn't happen to Richnuck or Adolph?"

I saw now what he was. This studio head could fit his compassion into his suit's breast pocket.

"Aren't you curious," I asked, "why these deaths happened so close together?"

"No! And you shouldn't be either! That's why I pay Manly!"

"To hush things up?" I asked, feigning innocence.

"Of course! Do you know what this kind of publicity could do to Mammoth? One word to Louisa Persons, and we might as well publish it in *Variety* and the *Reporter!*"

I stared at Lenski, who seemed to fade into his dark wood paneling. Before I could answer, he rose from his mammoth chair, came around, and perched himself on a desk whose legs were four carved lions.

"Mrs.—"

"Miss. Forenza."

He gave a cold smile.

"Even better. How much would it take for you to give up this case?"

Well. When you were head of a studio, you got right down to business.

"I'm not sure there's a price. See, I have this strange trait: I like to see justice done."

"*Justice?!*" Lenski snorted, his short legs dangling just above the carpet. "Save that for the pictchas, sweetheart!"

"Very well, Mr. Lenski. You've made your stance clear." I checked my watch. "I believe my five minutes are up."

Behind the cheaters, his eyes widened, and I watched him grip the fabric of his double-breasted suit.

"Are you all right?" I asked, running up to steady him.

His breathing, now labored, returned to a normal flow.

"Don't worry," he said with a wave. "It's just my heart acting up."

Errol had told me Lanski's pump went blooey whenever money came up.

I let go of his padded shoulder, damping down a smirk.

"Don't worry," I told him, turning for the long walk back. "I won't hit you up for a penny."

From behind, I heard a sigh of relief.

"And, Miss Forenza," he said, his tone back to 'kind grandpa' mode. "Don't forget to eat a bowl of my dear mama's chicken soup. For thirty-five cents, you shouldn't go hungry!"

"I've had it," I said over my shoulder, "and it was delicious."

Once outside, I motioned to Errol, and we entered the elevator. By the time we hit the lobby, we heard the loud clatter of heels before the staircase door banged open.

"Wait!" Scheherazade panted. She moved closer, dropping her voice. "Mr. Lenski just got a call. There's been another . . . accident."

I looked at Errol.

"Who is it this time?" I asked.

"A DP," she said. "Fell off a crane." She thrust a white envelope at me. "This is from the boss. He wants you to stay on the case."

With a last pant, she called the elevator. Errol and I stepped outside.

"What's a DP?" I asked.

"Director of Photography." I'm sure I looked blank. "I'll have you know, it's a very important job. He determines the overall look of a film, and is really more of an artist—"

"If he wasn't pushed from that crane," I said, "I'm the whole cast of *The Women*."

We followed a slow-rolling cart full of workers (most of whom whistled) and asked about the latest "accident."

"It was on 'New York Street,'" said one. "Hey, sister, how'd you like to go to the top of the Empire State with me?"

More catcalls followed.

"No thanks," I said. "I have a meeting with Murder Inc."

They all laughed. Then Errol and I worked our way to the front of the lot. As always, I couldn't have cared less about all those sets or fake streets next to real ones. I ignored where Tarzan had swung and where phony boats now sailed. Errol, of course, had to be towed every step.

As we passed yet another façade, it got me to thinking. The Mammoth execs seemed as hollow as backless sets. They'd turn a blind eye to anything—even murder—as long as the dream machine rolled. Who could wonder that with men like Manly in charge, the moral code at the studio was slightly below a whorehouse.

By the time we reached "New York Street," I could barely walk on my heels. Sheesh, this place was huge! And there was another, just-as-gargantuan lot stationed across the street! As I caught my breath beneath an old-fashioned lamppost, I saw a painter go by, bucket hanging from his bike's handlebars.

"Excuse me?" I called.

He stopped carefully.

"What can I do for you, dollface?"

There was nothing worse for a woman than being compared to a doll. Still . . .

"I understand a DP was just killed here. Do you know where exactly?"

"Sure," the grizzled guy nodded. "Wes Haskell. News spreads fast around here. Take a right at the fake drugstore and another by the fake 'Macy's.' Think the crane is still there."

"Thanks," I waved, moving off with Errol.

It seemed these Hollywood types, I thought, *the ones without fancy offices, fame, or Oscars were actually pretty decent.* It wasn't until you got to the top of the food chain that the fish began to smell.

Passing "Macy's," I looked around, not seeing a red light or crew. It was probably too hopeful to think a production had stopped to mourn. Most likely, they'd moved to another location. I stopped before a huge crane, its body crisscrossed with metal as it reached for the L.A. sky. It was anchored in place by a kind of cart—like the ones you'd see on train tracks—and the line of lights below made me think of Felize.

I looked down. The sun hurt my eyes. I tried to imagine the scene: this now-deserted street bustling with men in suits, each performing a different task, as they stared at Haskell behind a huge camera, reels sticking up like mouse ears, ready to go for a shot. Then—POOF!—he was gone, a broken form on the asphalt which couldn't be fixed by Electrical. Such grisly thoughts made me shudder: in my whole career, I'd never seen a dead body. And why would I? All my cases had stopped short of murder—until I'd entered Mammoth.

Errol and I bent down to examine the scene. We could still see faint splotches of blood despite the hosed-down concrete. If Haskell had "fallen" from where the crane was set now, he had about as much chance of surviving as me leaping off (the real) Chrysler Building.

Even in the L.A. sun, I shivered. I thought about questioning witnesses, but in this glare, they probably couldn't see Haskell much less a hand that pushed. I straightened and looked at Errol.

"That's *three* union guys gone. What would anyone have against them?"

"Maybe," he said, "they were rabble-rousers. Wanted to work less than six days a week."

I thought this over.

"Not bad. Tell you what: go around the lot and find some union reps. If they don't know, no one does."

He nodded, trotting off briskly. I stayed at the scene, trying to puzzle things out. Could it be Mrs. Felize? Manly? Or someone completely unknown? I sat on a stoop, pretending to be in Manhattan. Someday, I'd have to go. When Errol returned an hour later, we'd both had enough of the sun.

"Well?" I asked.

He shook his head.

"None of the stiffs was trouble. I talked to the reps, and they said all three were good guys. They got along with everyone—even the bosses. So that's one theory blown."

"Listen," I said. "Let me drop you off at my joint. I need some time to think."

"No sweat. Speaking of which, I need to take a shower."

And with that, we trundled back to the Ford.

Chapter 18
Manly's Boys

After Errol stepped out at the Proctor, I drove to Sontag's, ordered a coffee, and slumped over the counter. My mind was so full of the case, I was surprised my skull didn't expand. I had no new ideas—just another stiff. But I *did* have Lenski's cash, prodding the envelope to make sure. And, until we found the killer, I knew I could always draw from the Mammoth well. One thing, at least, to be thankful for.

You know what comes next.

I ride the elevator to my floor, a cold gat in my back as I have "fun" with two goons. Ever since Errol walked in, still dripping and dressed in a towel, one seems a bit crispy, while the other is down and groaning, clutching his privates like they were jewels.

"You tell Manly," I spat, "Nicky Forenza don't scare that easily. Not from second-rate hoods who get beat by a dame and an actor."

"Manly knows," the older guy gasped from the floor. He and I both glanced at his friend whose suit was still smoking.

"Knows what?" I bent as far down as was safe in my somewhat tight skirt.

"That ain't no actor—it's a dragon. Manly had the studio egghead do a little research."

I winced.

Did this probable withered librarian, poring over his picture books, know how much trouble he'd caused?

"Well, Jack," I said, "Manly may have his secrets, but I have mine. Tell him I know about Harlow's husband, and how Lenski walked off with evidence. If I stay hushed, so does Manly. He sends one more goon around and I tell my boyfriend—who happens to be a cop."

The guy laughed through his pain.

"Like Manly can't put the bite on."

"Not on this one. Amazing, I know, but he's honest."

"Well," said the hood, "Blow me down! An honest-to-God square bull!"

"You tell Manly. If you or him or the studio four-eyes squawks, trust me, I'll send you all over."

The hood grimaced.

"You got a deal. Now swear fire-lungs there won't breathe, and I'll just see myself out."

Still gripping his privates, he limped through the shattered door.

Errol narrowed his eyes.

"Can we trust him?" he asked.

"I think so. It's Manly I'm worried about. Anyway, we need to get rid of . . . this pile, this ash." I reached beneath my sink, grabbing two trash bags to hand them over. "Bag up what's left and dump it out of town. No way it can be ID'd."

"Yes, ma'am," said Errol, drying off to put on his suit before scooping up ashes. "I'll take the "N" to the Valley."

"Good," I nodded. "Nothing there but orange and lemon groves."

I threw off my heels—*a relief!*—to step shakily into my "kitchen." There, from a small drawer, I pulled out a half-empty bottle of Scotch. If today didn't merit a stiff drink, I was best pals with Manly.

Chapter 19
Death on the Backlot

The next morning, after Errol slept on the couch and I rolled off my rollaway bed, I decided to do something risky: go back to Mammoth. *It might be suicide,* I thought, slipping on some comfortable heels. Then again, I could find some clue to help me unravel this case. Or was that "cases"? At this point, I didn't know.

Once I'd emerged from my cubbyhole, fully dressed, a delightful smell hit my nostrils. I looked toward the kitchen and saw Errol, in his suit, singing some Dinah Shore torch song as he cooked eggs on my hotplate!

"Errol!" I cried, "since when do you cook?"

He grinned.

"I listened to *Betty Crocker*. She says eggs are fun and fluffy!"

I took another whiff.

"Indeed they are."

After a few cups of joe and Errol's extremely well-prepared fried eggs, we headed back to the Ford. I looked at the windshield. Another parking ticket. As always, I tore it in two, but deposited it in my ashtray. I might be a criminal, but I didn't want to litter.

Errol stayed quiet during the short drive to Mammoth. Maybe yesterday's jaunt to the Valley had worn him out. In any case, my old friend the guard was happily on duty and I slid into a Visitor's spot, legit pass secured. As I stepped out onto the running board, and then asphalt, I was grateful for my low heels. But then a mob of people ran toward us like Tarzan was on their tail. Curious, Errol and I joined them, smothered by the heat of well-dressed bodies. We clattered down "New York," passed its elevated station, and came to a halt at the shore of that big lake. What was going on? It felt like *Day of the Locust!* But as I shouldered my way up front, I saw this fake lake held something very real: a floating body! It was a man on his back, blue suit drenched, and arms flung out to his sides. But this paled beside what was wrapped around his throat: I could swear it looked like . . . film.

Number Four, I thought, straightening, and this is *not* a coincidence. A brave bunch of union guys waded into the water, which looked deep but really wasn't. Carefully, they floated the corpse to the shore, pulling it onto the dirt. All around me, women screamed and cried. Security showed up, shouting, "All right! Move on now!" but the celluloid-choked body was too great an attraction.

I pushed closer to stare down at the poor fellow. His face was blue, and I saw that tucked into his deadly collar was a small, folded note. Making sure I was quick, I crouched to retrieve it. Once I moved behind a tree, I opened its soaking folds.

"Don't be greedy," it read in even typewritten letters.

What the hell did that mean, I wondered, *and who was it meant for?*

Not wanting to pull a Lenski, I replaced the note where I'd found it when a voice behind me spoke up.

"It's Patrick Magee," I heard. "He was a picture cutter. Been here since the Silents."

Hmm. Another old-timer, deprived of a nice death in bed.

Transportation rolled in, lifting the dripping Magee and shoving him into the back of an open truck. Everyone else stayed still, horrified by what they'd seen and imagining what they hadn't.

"Okay, back on the job!" a dark-haired, dark-suited man commanded. He turned around.

"Mr. Manly?" I asked, striding up with Errol. I lowered my voice. "Don't you think this has gone far enough?"

"Ah, the lady dick. And her 'actor' sidekick." He turned to Errol. "Tell me—what picture are you on?"

I thought quickly.

"Beneath the Land of Oz," I said.

Manly laughed, but the sound was not friendly. He shooed away everyone near us.

"Good one, Miss Forenza."

"Call me Nicky," I said.

"Call me Mr. Manly. Didn't Meir tell you to scram? And my two boys—"

"—now sadly one," I added.

"Yeeees," he drawled, with an almost feral look. "And did they not convey the message that you need to butt out?"

"Oh, they did," I said, "but one is now fertilizing citrus."

"I don't take kindly to you blipping one of my boys," Manly growled.

"And *I* don't kindly to being poked by iron. Especially at my own door."

We stared at each other, his olive face bristling, until he took a step forward.

"Take the hint," he said. "Stay off the lot before you join Little Tony."

"I don't understand you," I said, refusing to be cowed. "A whole host of people saw that poor cutter's body. And, as we know, studio folk *do* talk. You might want to cover up this one, but *four* deaths in one week? It's bound to make the *Examiner*."

He gave a thin-lipped smile.

"Oh, I don't think so."

"Is there anyone in this town you and Lenski don't own?"

His smile broadened.

"Not really. Picture money's spread *all over* this town."

"Like manure?"

He glowered.

"Look, I won't out that beast—" he stuck a stubby finger at Errol, "—if you agree to leave here and never come back." He fumbled with his wallet. "How does five grand sound?"

"Like a lot of money," I said, "but unfortunately, I can't take it."

"A regular Girl Scout, huh?" Manly clenched his beefy fists. "Well, Saint Nicky, we have ways of getting to you. Ways even you can't imagine."

"Going to reveal my secret love nest with Brock Powell?"

Now Manly advanced again, his short frame towering over me.

"Smart broads get dead," he growled. "Especially those who screw with the studios."

"Lucky for me," I said, "that Mr. Lenski has assigned me to this case."

Manly nearly went white.

"What?"

"Yes, it was the third 'accident' that changed his mind. Mr. Manly, aren't you going to welcome me to Mammoth?"

Errol snorted.

"Button it, dragon," growled Manly.

Errol stepped up to him, utterly without fear.

"I want you to know," he said, "you so much as touch one unpainted nail of Nicky's, and I'm going to show you Hell." His yellow eyes became slits. "The one with the scorching flames."

Manly stood his ground.

"Well, you're heading there now. Only, you don't know it."

"Remember," I said, "Mr. Lenski."

"Yeah yeah," muttered Manly, stalking off no doubt to threaten some gossip columnists.

I turned to Errol.

"He's right," I said. "Hollywood *is* Hell."

Chapter 20
Don't Screw with a Studio

Manly's next move wasn't subtle—even compared to sending two goons to scare me.

"I don't like this," said Errol, ducking to enter the Ford. "Remember Thomas Ince?"

"Who?"

"The bird who allegedly fell from Hearst's yacht. Hollywood covered it up."

"Right," I said from behind the wheel. In case we were being tailed, I went out the Culver Gate, past Selznick Studios, its column-fronted façade a dead ringer for Tara. In fact, it *was* Tara.

"That's the legend," said Errol, rolling his eyes. "What really happened: Ince left that yacht and died a few days later. Rumor has it Hearst suspected his mistress was making out with Chaplin, and shot Ince by mistake."

"Who was his actual target?"

"Chaplin, his mistress, or both."

"Hooray for Hollywood."

"That's my point," Errol said. He looked worried. "You run up against guys like Lenski and Manly, and suddenly find yourself dead." He tensed. "I think I should carry a gun."

I laughed as I turned onto Highland, ignoring a blaring horn.

"Why on earth would you need one?"

"What if they come after you?"

I laughed.

"Errol, you're a dragon—you've got nasty claws and a tail, not to mention you breathe fire. Don't you think that's enough?"

"I'm not sure," he said, biting a talon. "A pill moves faster than I do."

"True. But you'd need a gun permit. Plus, you're not trained."

"Were you?" he asked. "When you broke open that gas case?"

"Well, no. But I have hands. Holding a gun comes naturally. Like, uh, spewing fire does for you."

"Hmph."

He crossed his arms, not speaking the whole way back to Hollywood. I thought we could go home, make some joe, and relax. Like most of life, it didn't turn out like I planned. I pulled the Ford to the curb, stepping out into traffic. As if that wasn't enough, I felt the cold prod of steel in my back.

"Not again," I groaned.

"That's right, sister," said a man, and the voice was familiar. Very slowly, I craned my neck to see the goon who'd barely escaped with his manhood.

"Haven't you had enough?" I asked.

"Nope. Manly don't seem to think so."

"So it's back upstairs?"

"Not this time, sweetheart. Get in the jalopy. You, dragon, get out."

He escorted me to the passenger side as Errol stepped onto the sidewalk. Errol let out a frightening growl.

"Now, now," said the hood, "one spark and the dame gets it."

Errol closed his mouth.

I might be out of traffic, but I was hardly safe. That insistent muzzle kept poking until I slid over cracked vinyl. The hood, damn him, pirated my bag, tucking it into his jacket.

Confident I was helpless, he turned back to Errol.

"You—dragon boy." He kept his heater on me. "C'mere."

Though Errol's eyes blazed, he listened. Manly's boy removed a pair of snappers and cuffed them around my friend's claws. Across his back. Then it was time for his legs, which he wrapped in a tight yellow rope.

"What do you want?" I snarled, as he gestured for the keys. I threw them at his head, but he caught them like Yogi Berra, easing into the driver's seat.

As the old engine roared to life, I turned my head to see Errol standing helpless. His roars reached even me as my captor cruised down the boulevard."

"Just relax, Nicky," he said. "This ain't gonna be long."

"Where are we going?" I asked.

"You'll see."

I decided to get friendly.

"Got a name?"

"Eddie."

"So the gang you're part of is jake with abducting women?"

"You know the rules. When Manly says do, I do. Even pushing a baby buggy right down Angel's Flight."

"You're a real sweetheart, Eddie."

He grinned.

"I'm about to show you how much."

I was careful to pay attention to where he steered the Ford. I watched him get onto Cahuenga and head into the Valley.

"You got a thing for citrus?" I asked.

"I'm allergic."

"Then what are we doing going past all these groves?"

He turned to me and grinned.

"Patience, Nicky. I'm gonna take you to a place you'll like. Real pretty."

I looked out the window. Now we were going through cropland—oddly surrounded by palm trees with an occasional house or two, a broken-down tractor, but no actual people. Now *I* was getting allergic—to this whole situation. Guys like Eddie rejoiced in taking enemies "for a ride"—from which they never returned. I had no gun. I had no weapon. Even my heels were flat. If I couldn't think my way out of this, I'd meet my end in the Valley. And nobody wanted that.

"Last stop," crowed Eddie, shutting off the Ford. Frankly, I was shocked it'd made it *this* far. His automatic still trained on me, Eddie got out and circled the hood, yanking my door open to forcibly shove me out. Once I steadied, I surveyed the lay of the land. We were by a railway station—not like Union Station downtown, but small and quaint, like something from the Old West. The small building was two stories and boasted a mounted weathervane.

"Where is this?" I asked. "Which part of the Valley?"

"Northridge," he smirked. "Just a sleepy small town. Lucky *City of Los Angeles* is due any minute."

I stiffened. Was Manly *really* this cruel? Was his hood going to ice me in a scene straight out of Hollywood?

Eddie adjusted his hat, seizing me by the arm and dragging me over dirt. I felt like a sack of grain.

"Manly's orders," he told me cheerfully as he pushed me the few feet to the tracks.

"Please," I said as he wrestled me to the ground, procured a rope from his jacket, and proceeded to tie me up—to the tracks! "Didn't this go out with the Silents?" I asked. But there I was, like Little Nell, at the mercy of a villain who lacked only a twirling cape. "Really?" My captor nodded, grinning. "Even *Manly* can't be this cliché. I'm surprised he didn't send the Wicked Witch!"

"That's you, sweetheart," said Eddie, eyes shining with accomplishment. "What a shame: the lady dick, heartsick over some bird, drives into the Valley and decides to end her own life."

Even though this situation was dire, I laughed.

"Did I tie myself up, too?"

"Nobody did. Bye, baby. Not been nice knowin' you." He checked his watch. "Better blow this pop stand." Whistling his way to my Ford, he drove off in a dust cloud. I saw a couple of tumbleweeds tumbling in his wake.

Now what? How did Little Nell manage to escape the mustachioed villain? Of course. She had help. The hero would come riding up, freeing her from her bonds.

I was my own hero.

Rubbing the rope which secured my wrists against the smooth metal track, I hoped friction would work before I became trainkill. The Northridge sun was fierce—adding a good ten degrees to the temperature in the city— but I never stopped trying: not even when I heard a whistle which wasn't so far away.

I wouldn't let Hollywood kill me! I thought, stepping up (or wristing up) my efforts. Now I heard the smooth progress of wheels, the chug-chug-chug of the engine. A yellow locomotive was now hurtling toward me. But the instinct to cling to life—which we all have—kept me rubbing that rope. As *The City of Los Angeles* tried to come to a screeching halt, black smoke pouring from its wheels and funnel, my hands sprang free. The engineer had seen the obstacle—*me*—but there wasn't even a slim chance he'd be able to stop in time. I said a silent prayer: hoped my family—and Bill—would remember the good me.

This piety came to a halt by a rush of wind so strong I could no longer see through my hair. Then I felt myself lifted, dangling high above those tracks as the yellow engine streaked by. Though afraid to open my eyes, as a sleuth I was naturally curious.

I forced my lids to lift, seeing my jacket clutched in two claws with six-inch long black talons. I repressed an urge to cheer.

"Errol," I asked, "however did you find me?"

He thrust down his spiked head.

"I'll save it for later. For now, let's just fly."

Chapter 21
Ma Chimes In

We did. With the Valley sun so bright, and the people so sparse, I could swear we wouldn't be seen. And even if we were, it would be written off as a hoax: another *War of the Worlds*. Since I was afraid to look down, I kept my eyes straight ahead—on the rural, crop-filled landscape. The sight of sheep grazing added to my calm. At least, that's what I told myself.

I craned my neck up.

"Don't drop me," I begged Errol as he veered south toward L.A. "Also, I think we should take a red car lickety-split before we're spotted."

"Yes, boss!" he grinned, gliding in a sky so clear it practically hurt your eyes. After a few minutes, he smoothly dropped down to Lankershim and a nearby streetcar stop.

"Phew," I said as he set me down gently. "That was quite a ride! How much?"

Errol adjusted his hat. Miraculously, it still sat on his head.

"For you only, no charge."

"I can't thank you enough!" I told him. "If it weren't for you, I'd be swimming with the—"

"—Caboose?" he finished. He looked down at his claws. "Feeling's mutual. You took me in and cared for me when you didn't have to."

"Remember those twenty-five G's?"

"There's more to it. Besides, you gave me a swell job—and you *trust* me."

"I . . ." I couldn't deny it, but I didn't want to go soft. "Well, don't let it go to your head."

He patted mine, hair so wild from our flight I must have looked like Einstein. I smoothed down a few curls so someone wouldn't ask me about $E=mc^2$. Then we both heard the jangle of a red car approaching. The driver in his white shirtsleeve was too polite to refuse us entry. We must have made quite a pair.

Once we moved past shocked passengers, with me mumbling, "the movies," we plopped ourselves in the back, both in a stew to leave the Valley behind. At least, *I* certainly was.

"So." I turned to Errol. "Start chirping. How did you escape and find me?"

He settled in, crossing his legs in front of him.

"If that cheap hood," he said, "thought he could stop me with ropes, he was all wet."

I looked at him expectantly. "That dumbbell forgot I have *claws*. And my talons are long enough—" he held a pointed one out, "—to reach up to that twine and bust it. Once I was free, I followed your car."

"How?"

"With these, silly." He ruffled his furled wings.

"But I never saw you."

"No kidding—the Valley sun is brighter than you are." I smacked his shoulder. "That's why I lost you. But I picked up your trail in the nick of time."

"A thrilling Hollywood ending."

He bounced up from his seat.

"Aren't those the best kind?!"

I put a hand on his claw.

"Errol, you're more than a peach—you're the whole damn orchard! And I swear, I'll never forget this."

"I think you will." He winked. "Next time you're with Bill."

When we finally got back to the office, I picked up the phone to ring Bill.

"What gives?" he asked in his friendly bass.

"Where are you?"

"At the station. Where are *you?*"

"Bill, it's a long story, but my Ford's been nicked."

He stifled a chuckle.

"Who'd want it?"

"Guy named Eddie—the one who might not have children, thanks to me."

"Where was he last spotted?"

"Northridge. Burning rubber away from the station."

"On it." I heard the crackle of a two-way radio. "Don't sweat it, Nicky. We'll get that old machine back."

"And Eddie?"

"Hope he enjoys his time in the slammer."

I exhaled.

"Thanks. I owe you."

I could hear the grin in his voice.

"I'll hold you to that. Bye."

Once I put down the horn, I slumped into my office, taking a seat on the desk. Errol was right behind me.

"This has been quite a day," I said.

"That's one way to put it. Want me to put on some joe?"

"Errol, you're an angel."

"Really more of a dragon."

He went out and clattered around, which resulted in the heavenly scent of beans mixing with water.

"Here you go."

He handed me a mug, and for a long minute, we sipped away in silence.

"What's it all about?" I asked, expecting an answer to this as fast as to, "So who *is* Santa Claus, really?"

"Duck soup," Errol shrugged. "Manly acts fast. He wants you—forgive the pun—out of the picture."

"He nearly got his wish." I could still hear that ghost whistle—the rumble of wheels on the track. "I mean, I know why he's after me—but why the birds at Mammoth? Why would he off an editor?"

"Beats me. Too many closeups on the cutting room floor?"

"Ha." I thought back to that note. "I found something—hanging from Magee's necklace. It said, 'Don't be greedy.' What do you think that means?"

"Maybe he wasn't happy with his pay. Although I understand editors—"

"—That doesn't explain the others. All of them were old-timers just doing their job." I leaned forward. "Why would you kill a guy who pulls cables? Or adjusts the lights on a set?"

Errol shook his head.

"Personal grudge?"

"Maybe." I kicked at my lower desk. "Errol, I'm stumped. And—forgive the pun—you've earned your wings today. Why don't you head for home?"

"I don't have one," he said, looking down. "Remember?"

"Yes you do, and you have the key."

"It's jake. Think I'll catch the end of Bob Hope."

"I wish someone would."

After he left, the ameche jingled.

"Nicky Forenza, Private Eye," I heard Errol intone. Then a shouted, "Nicky, it's your boyfriend!"

That rare blush crept over my cheeks as I lifted my office receiver. I heard a little buzz. "Hang up, Errol!" There was a click.

"Bill, I hope you didn't hear that."

"The hang up or the boyfriend?"

"Both."

"I did. And I must say I'm flattered."

The heat from my cheeks nearly felled me.

"Enough with the kidding. What's shaking?"

"Well, Van Nuys caught friend Eddie and he's still enjoying the Valley. Those bulls'll drive the old girl to you and hand over the keys."

"Bill, you're a prince!"

"Not me. Maybe one of my Viking cousins."

"Please make sure Van Nuys asks about Manly."

"Will do, but I doubt Eddie'll squawk."

I doubted it too. You wanted to cross Manly like you did Leo the Lion.

Thinking of Mammoth, a plan clicked into place as smoothly as a safe's tumbler.

"Hey, Bill," I said, "I had such a great time at Ciro's, thought we might try Mocambo's." Then I remembered the one good dress in my closet and how fast it could be cleaned. "Would-would tomorrow night work?"

"Sure. I'll swing by at eight. And Nicky—?" I froze. "Don't get too close to a train."

I laughed.

"See you then."

"Want me to run to the dry cleaner?"

I looked up, spotting Errol, freed from Hope's corny gags.

"Sure," I said, "that's swell! Let me give you some dough." I fumbled in my bag. "You still have your house key?"

"Gee, Nicky," he said, "I didn't know you cared!"

"No need to sugar me." I passed some coins into his waiting claw. "Now scram!"

I sighed. *Where did that leave me?* Since I had time to kill, I decided to visit Ma.

I took the "N" line down the boulevard, hopping off before the Egyptian. Some flick I'd never heard of blared its title at me, but I ignored the blood-red sign, meant to resemble—*what?*—a pharaoh's boat? I took a quick right, striding down two blocks by instinct. Small, unobtrusive houses lined the crowded streets, only the distant "HOLLYWOODLAND" sign providing a hint of glamor. Otherwise, the union guys—like Larry and Anthony and Patrick—made up the bulk of the neighborhood.

When I got to Ma's, I didn't knock—just pushed open the door. Not much had changed since my childhood: maybe a new lamp or pillow, but for the most part, the décor was strictly 30's—with a bit of the 20's thrown in.

"MA!" I yelled, the comfort of being home and with my own kind turning me more Italian.

"Nicky?" Mom asked from the kitchen as she stirred a savory pot.

"Who you cookin' for?"

"Just me and the boys," she grabbed me in a hug. All my memories of her seem to be shrouded in steam. She untied her apron, opening the fridge to take out some homemade Sfogliatella and sliding a plate toward me.

"Mangia, mangia, figlio mio!" she cried.

"Okay, Ma, you don't have to twist my arm." Once I'd swallowed rich ricotta, I brought up the dreaded subject.

"Heard anything from Pops?"

She sighed, walking over to a wood cabinet and lifting up a creased paper.

"I got this today." She unfolded the paper and read:

Dear Angela:

Hope you are well. Me and Giuseppe are doing good.

The Feds are still treating us right, though all my thoughts are with you. Tell Nicky & the boys not to worry—this war will be over soon.

All My Love,

Pops

"I don't believe a word!" I spat angrily. "Must have been worked over by the censor!"

"Still, it's something."

After a year, the sting of Pops' detainment had settled to a low buzz.

"Why don't they let him go?" I asked, stabbing my pastry. "Didn't Roosevelt say we Italians are jake?"

"That's *President* Roosevelt. And you know California. Always have to look tough."

"I hate Warren, and DeWitt, and that bastard Hoover! Fencing us up and the Japanese like we were livestock!"

Ma sighed, digging into her own dessert.

"*Mia figlia,* that's war. After Pearl Habor, they think we're hiding planes in the fridge."

I slammed down my fist, burning for Pops and Guiseppe, but also Matsuka, my dormmate at UCLA. Word on the street was that she was taken for the crime of being herself. *And not only her, but her parents, had all been born in L.A.!*

"This war could go on forever," I growled. "The Krauts are on the move."

Ma waved a dismissive hand.

"Let them," she said. "They won't win. Everyone is against them, and 'Il Dulce' is a joke."

"So is Hitler," I spat. "Just a much more dangerous one."

We finished up in silence, but I knew what was coming next. I filled my mouth with cream so I could delay my answer.

"Well," said Ma, raising a brow like mothers everywhere. "You meet any nice boys?"

I mimed not being able to talk, but at some point I had to swallow.

"All the nice boys," I told her, "are in uniform and gone."

Ma clucked her tongue.

"What about that tall policeman?"

"It just so happens," I said, "he's taking me out tomorrow."

Ma gave a strangled sigh, a strange mix of joy and sorrow. When it came to shame, she was better than a priest.

"Ehi! At this point, I guess he's better than nothing."

I gleefully took up Ma's old argument.

"But, Ma, he's blond and he's not Italian and he's from Swedish stock. Worse—" I hastily crossed myself, "—he's not a Catholic!"

"At least he believes in Our Lord."

I got up to pour us some coffee.

"Yeah, I guess he does."

"How's work?" she asked, deftly changing the subject.

"Not great," I sighed. "Can't really discuss it, but let's say it's sprinkled with stardust."

"Don't you get involved with those Jews!"

"Ma, religion has nothing to do with it. It's just that show biz has the basic morals of a whore."

"Nicky!" Ma cried, scandalized.

On that note, I better go. If Ma knew I was mixed up in murder and hoods like Manly and Eddie, lighting twelve candles in church would be too few to soothe her.

"You take care," I told her, walking around to hug her sitting form. Our people don't stand on ceremony.

"Never mind me!" she cried, flinging her arms back to embrace mine. "You watch out for yourself!"

"I will," I said, accepting from her some fresh pastries tied into a box with string.

Ma had one golden rule, and she didn't learn it at Mass: God forbid you should leave her house hungry.

Chapter 22
Dancing the Night Away

The next day, I didn't do much more than brood: about the case, Pops... even Bill.

Tonight, I vowed, *I would find out where I stood.* I was either a very good friend or some untouchable goddess. Frankly, I didn't like either option.

Errol had retrieved The Dress for me from our local cleaner's, and he looked so proud he nearly burst through his vest. He'd even gone back to Beverly Hills to score some *borrowed* jewelry.

That night, I asked, "Isn't this kind of pathetic?" as he tried, with his awkward claws, to clasp shut a thick diamond necklace.

"No!" he insisted. "Tiffany and Harry Winston want their gems to be seen."

"And then returned?" I chuckled. "Good luck with that."

"I told them you're jake. You're on the side of the law."

"Mostly," I grinned. "Here, let me," I said, reaching around my gold straps. With jewels in place, I whirled before my largest mirror—the one which barely reflected my face. "How do I look?" I asked, jitters assaulting me.

"Like a queen!" Errol enthused. "Even better, *like a star!*"

I thought of the dress' history.

"A second-hand one, at least."

Errol waved a claw at the door, his own suit, thank the Lord, newly cleaned and pressed.

"You better get down there," he said.

I nodded, practicing walking on five-inch heels as I clomped to the elevator. The doors opened.

"Bill," I greeted my date who looked yummy in his dark suit. I felt better, since I wasn't the only one who had to repeat an outfit.

"You look exquisite," he smiled, bending to kiss the back of my hand. Good thing the telephone girl was off, since I don't carry smelling salts.

"So do you," I said, gathering all my courage. *No blushing,* I told myself. "Shall we?"

He bowed, leading me out to another borrowed machine: a blue Ford De Luxe heavy on the chrome.

I got in, smoothing down those heavy gold beads. *How did these actresses do it?*

There was a rare awkward silence, and to fill it, I asked, "Any peeps from my pal Eddie?"

"Not one. Turns out he's a Harpo." He turned to me with a grin. "So—why Mocambo's?"

"Errol says it's really swinging."

"Well, then it must be."

It was just a short jog back to the Strip. A left on North Laurel, a right on Sunset, and we followed the sizzle of neon to another bland building. As with Ciro's, only the name was lit, but the line of Rollses out front revealed the joint's secret: it was a Hollywood playground. After Bill pressed some coins into a waiting palm, he took my arm and we went in. I thought I'd landed in Cuba!

The club was a knockout: LIVE BIRDS squawked from glass cages lining every walls. A Latin theme gave way to pillars striped like candy canes, and from the bandstand I heard a smooth voice much like Sinatra's. It was hard to move, and not just on the dance floor: hordes of women in gowns and men in suits and bowties crowded not only tables but the narrow spaces between them. The languorous drawl of voices—"filled with money," as F. Scott would have it—created a swell of sound like a P-38 taking off.

"This must be the place to be," I said to Bill after a waiter had pulled out my chair. Once we were seated, he ordered something French and I leaned over to speak. *Not too far,* I cautioned. "See anyone you know?" I grinned.

"Well . . ." His eyes scanned the bustling room, "I see a few folks from pictures, but . . ." He stopped. "Am I off my rocker, or is that your Mrs. Felize?"

I froze. By God, there she was, brazen as any starlet, couture gown hugging her assets, and this time . . . she clinked glasses with somebody new! This dame sure got around, and for a new widow, her smile was oddly cheerful.

"Good evening," I told her, after I'd fought my way through the crowd. She looked up at me with surprise, then covered it with disdain.

"Same dress, huh?" she asked. "Guess my dough didn't go far."

"Speaking of dough—" I nodded over her gown. "—looks like you got yours. Insurance pay out like a slot?"

"None of your beeswax," she smirked. "Oh." She gestured to her new guy: this one was prettier than the last, his wavy black hair and moustache stand-ins for Brock Powell's. "This is Lloyd Richardson," Felize smirked. "You must have seen him in *Angels Don't Have Wings.*"

"Sorry," I nodded as he started to rise. "Please, don't get up. I'm afraid I'm not big on pictures."

"I hope to be," he rejoined, his mid-Atlantic accent probably hiding some Southern drawl.

"Good for you," I said, noting their bottle of wine. French. Pricey. "So," I directed at her, "when was poor Larry at last put to rest?"

She looked bored.

"Sunday. Why do you ask?"

"Well, just curious if he's still fresh and able to view your new beau."

Her eyes lit up with danger.

"What do you mean? He's dead!"

"I know. I meant from the other world."

With a smile worthy of Carrie, I sashayed away in my copy of her gown.

"Well?" Bill asked, once I'd seated myself.

"She's moved up. In taste and in men."

"You still don't think she's a suspect?"

I sipped our own wine. It was good.

"Not sure. I can see why she'd like Larry dead, but the other three? Unless she was named in their wills, why bother knocking them off?"

Bill raised his big hands to shrug.

"Beats me. Hey." He pointed down at the menu. "You like this lobster thermidor, right?"

"Actually, it was newburg. But I tend to like lobster in general since my chances to eat it are slim."

Bill gave me a wink.

"Maybe that'll change."

Damn it! My cheeks flamed and I lifted a hand to cool them. Just then, an odd dancing couple—like a Munchkin and a giantess—halted their lively samba to stand over our table. I blinked. It was none other than Meir Lenski, and divesting herself from his arms—hell, even *I* knew her!—was Ingrid Johannson, the famed Swedish actress with a face like smooth carved marble. As Bill rose at her entrance, I tried not to stare.

"Mr. Lenski," I said with a nod. "And Miss Johannson. To what do we owe the pleasure?"

"Nothing good," snarled Lenski, snapping his fingers for two more chairs. The waiters, heedless of room, packed them in tightly. Since Lenski made no move to help his star take her seat, Bill performed this duty.

Was I wrong, I wondered, or did his eyes linger *a bit too much over her spangled gown?*

"Hey!" Lenski snapped to a waiter. "Two more glasses. Don't you know who I am?"

"Of course, Mr. Lenski!"

The waiter shot off like an U-boat as the studio head turned to me.

"I'm in a hole," he whined.

"What seems to be the matter?"

Meir pointed a finger at Ingrid.

"Her," he said in a low tone, causing me to suspect he thought a reporter might be disguised as a cockatoo.

"Mr. Lenski," I said, "You should know I'm not at all qualified to deal with Hollywood contracts or misbehaving stars—"

"For once, she ain't misbehaving!" he growled. I thought back to what Errol had said: that he'd gotten his start in the junk business. I waited. "Someone tried to ice her! Crashed a mirror in her dressing room and missed by this much!" He formed a tiny space with his thumb and forefinger.

"Try to calm down," I whispered. "Remember—your heart?"

"Fuck my heart!" he half-screamed, drawing attention from his many employees. He folded his hands, leaning forward. "You were right, Forenza. I should have listened to you—not that schmuck Manly!"

"You're not planning to cover this up?"

"How can I?" he hissed. "Killing grips and cutters is one thing, but when it comes to my stars—"

"'More than there are in Heaven'?"

"You betcha! And though they're a pain in my ass, I need them to live so they keep making ictchas!"

He refilled the glass which by now had been brought with a generous portion of wine. Ours.

I snuck a glance at Ingrid. Her face didn't move. She must have had work done.

"Mr. Lenski," I said, leaning forward as far as my dress would allow. "Can you think of anything—anything at all—connecting the four Mammoth victims and Miss Johannson?"

"Not offhand," he said, removing his glasses to wipe them. "Maybe they worked on her ictchas, but the crew keeps its distance from the talent."

I nodded. Just like a welder wouldn't walk up to FDR.

"That doesn't leave me with much."

"Let me leave you with this." Lenski reached into his jacket, removing an unmarked white envelope. Once he handed it over, I took a peek inside. *Mama mia!* Crammed with more C-notes than Manly had goons!

"I take it, Mr. Lenski, you want me to see this thing through."

He gave a thin-lipped smile.

"Of course. Find the guy, but discreet-like. No flashy headlines or—" he threw a cold glance at Bill, "—cops."

"You've been tailing me," I said.

"You should feel honored. Look, just find this *hmendrik* and hand him to me. I'll take care of the rest."

My eyes met Bill's. It went without saying I wanted to catch the killer, but I wanted to do it legit. And that meant involving the law.

"I'll do my best, Mr. Lenski. No guarantees. Just one more thing: call off Manly and his boys."

"Consider it done." He put a finger to his chin. "He might have to go out of town."

Not knowing if this trip would include a permanent ending, I nodded as Lenski and his star rose.

"I almost forgot," I said. "Can you put a ringer on Mammoth's schedule? Call it *Fire and Fame.*"

"Sounds meshuga, but all right." Before he and Ingrid took their place in a wild conga, he paused to look me over. "Nice dress," he said. "Carrie wore it splendidly."

"Holy mackerel!" Bill whistled as they whirled off. "That Johansson is stunning. Doesn't say much, though."

"Her face is too tight."

I opened my bag, cramming in the envelope so I now had two. This had been quite a night—and not the one I'd expected. Instead of kindling romance, it made me suspect Mrs. Felize and let me breathe easy as far as Manly. Thinking of Bill, I tried to brighten, digging into my lobster and later a luscious meringue, but my heart just wasn't in it.

Who *had bumped off four crewmen and attempted to rub out a star? What would motivate such a killer?*

I didn't feel much like dancing and Bill knew it. After paying the bill (which must have cost a month's salary), he led me out to the Ford—the nice one—and drove at a fast clip to Hollywood. Frankly, I was sick of it: both the town and the Industry.

After Bill escorted me into the lobby, *I* was the one to peck *his* cheek before making a quick exit. All my hopes for romance had gone up like so much kindling. I *had* to find the killer—get justice for those four stiffs—and unlike Mrs. Felize, for those who mourned their passing.

Chapter 23
The Lonely Dragon

Still buoyed by tonight's adventures, the blood in my ears beat Taps as I fitted my key to the lock. When I opened the door, I saw Errol sprawled across my couch, a pack of Camels on one side and a bottle of Bacardi on the other. He must have found my stash.

"Errol?" I asked softly, bending as much as I could in that dress. I threw down my mink and snapped off heavy earrings. Turned out diamonds weighed a lot.

I don't know if he heard me since all I got was a grunt. Then he belched in my face, his breath like a roomful of Hollywood writers. *Now* I was sore. I rolled him onto the carpet, filled the drained bottle with water, and splashed it into his face.

"Whatcha do for?" he slurred, trying to wipe his eyes with his claw. "Tryin' ruin every fun?"

I looked around my studio, wondering how this joint could ever be joined with "fun."

"I am not!" I shouted down to him.

"Sure. Easy you to say. Goin' out to Moca—Mocabomos."

"Macambo's. Errol, I thought we agreed you can't hit the clubs. No actor is *that* Method."

He sat up slightly, unbuttoning his jacket. His tie was wrapped around his head.

"Sure. 'Course," he said. "Leave the beastie a' home."

I shook my head.

"Errol, you seemed happy enough when I left. Don't you want to know what happened?"

His answer was a belch.

"Don' tell me. Don' matter. Only Bill an' Lenny."

"Lenski. And that's baloney! Of course you matter!"

"Naw." Now he was getting weepy. I half-expected a drunken, "I luv m' partner." Instead, he looked up and said: "I jus' a thing for smacks. Then, I the gutter." He gave a short laugh through his tears.

"What?" I knelt beside him like a beaded curtain that had abandoned its rack. "That's just the Bacardi talking. And maybe, at first, you're right, it was about the dough, but that hasn't been true for ages! You're—you're my partner, and you saved me from Manly's boys. Not to mention being hit by a train! If you hadn't come, I'd be flatter than Ma's lasagna!" He started to sniff and I offered a hankie. "Here." He blew loudly. "Feel better?" At first he nodded, then burst into guttural sobs.

"Errol! What is it?"

"I . . . I lonely," he sniffled. "Only dragon in town. Maybe whole world."

"But Errol, you have friends here! There's me, and Bill, and the telephone girl downstairs—"

"Not the same. No lady dragon."

His scaled shoulders shook.

I sighed. What could I say? I'd be a chump to think there were more of his kind up here.

"Tell you what." I tried to think clearly though I was overdressed. "Once we crack this case, we'll try to find a dame dragon."

"Really?" He gave such a hopeful look I wrapped my arms around his neck.

"Promise. Even if we have to go . . . to the center of the Earth."

Another loud blow before his yellow eyes widened.

"You'd do that for *me?*"

"Of course. You're my partner. And we do things for each other. What's more . . . you're my friend." When was the last time I'd said that? Fifth grade?

Errol wiped his eyes.

"That's the nicest thing ever!"

Now he was clawing my hands, talons an inch away from scratching me.

"Ease off!" I laughed. "We've both had a rough night. Let's hit the hay, and tomorrow, I'll tell you what happened with Felize."

"And Bill."

His head hit the carpet. As I unwrapped his tie, he started to snore like a . . . dragon.

The next morning, I heard groans coming from beneath the couch. I knew just what to do, dumping grounds in my paper filter, waiting for the orange light, and bringing a mug out to Errol.

"You're an angel," he breathed, sitting up to clutch his head. "Why am I the one with wings?"

I grinned, handing him the joe. He gulped it down faster than a bullet in flight.

"So . . . tell me," he demanded, yellow eyes unfogging.

"Mrs. Felize is quite the operator, but a killer? If it were just her husband, maybe. But with all these others..."

I got up to grab my own cup, the aroma alone delightful. Then I frowned.

"You seem down," Errol said. "I hope it's not me. I don't remember a lot from last night." I waved a hand. "Not me? Bill then?"

"Uh... not really." In the morning's harsh light, I knew I'd sent him the message to "Stay Away!" I let a warm sip of Joe slide down my throat. "It's this case. No one knows how all the murders connect—not even Lenski. And to make an attempt on the life of a major star—it almost makes me think our man is screwy."

"*What?*"

Errol snapped awake.

"Oh yeah. You know Ingrid Johannson? Her mirror tried to off her."

"A fitting end for an actress." I chuckled as Errol retrieved more joe. "Just remember—we don't know the killer's motive. To him, it all might make sense."

"Maybe," I sighed, lifting the one window to let in some air. I immediately wished I hadn't: the jangle of streetcars, constant honking of automobiles, and shouts from other "bachelors" made me slam it back down. "I do think we should fox around Ingrid's dressing room. Maybe our man left a clue."

"And maybe," said Errol, "I'm Carole Landis."

Chapter 24
Foxing Around

We were such regulars at the lot, we should have been given a permanent parking sticker. When the gate guard spotted our auto, he instantly scrawled out a pass.

"Say, do you know where the stars' dressing rooms are?" I asked out the open window.

"Toward the back," he said. "Take Main Street just past Stage 4."

"Thanks."

We ditched the old Ford in front of the stage. I shrugged. Let the pretend cops cite me: I happened to know a real one.

"This is it?"

Errol stared up at a short staircase, the building it led to squat, yellow, and old. I have to admit even *I* felt let down.

"Oh well," I said. "What'd you expect? A red carpet and wreaths of roses?"

"Uh . . ."

We consulted one of those boards you usually see in a lobby, only this time, the stick-on white letters held a different meaning: the names of top movie stars, lined up like tax accountants. I heard Errol's gasp and prepped myself to catch him—just in case he fell over.

We found the number matching "Ingrid Johansson" and I boldly went over and knocked. Answering the door was not Sweden's best import, but a mousy maid in uniform.

"Nicky Forenza," I said, digging around for my license.

She nodded.

"Come about the accident?" she opened the door wider. "It was horrible! Miss Johansson was nearly struck!"

"Or iced," I mumbled, hoping she hadn't heard.

"I am still cleaning up. Glass is just everywhere!"

"I take it no cops were called?"

"Oh no!"

She put her hands to her mouth, acting as if I'd asked if she'd seen Lenski naked. I motioned to Errol, leading him to what had been a lighted mirror. Now, shards of lights and glass littered the thick carpet. I stared at the counter below in wonder. This dame had more cosmetics than Estee Lauder at Bullock's. Might explain the look of that perfect face . . .

Errol and I both crouched to examine splinters which caught the L.A. sun. They didn't tell us much: A mirror had fallen and broken. *But how?*

I nodded my thanks to the maid, then jerked my head at my partner. We moved to the next room—the one sharing a wall with Ingrid's Make-up Emporium. I knocked. No answer. I tried the door—it opened. Strange. When I entered, Errol at my heels, I saw why. Vacant. No star from up above to spread her celestial rays. I went over to the wall adjoining Ingrid's, moving aside lush draperies and taking down a painting: of a smiling Lenski. Behind the now-empty spot was not faded paint but a hole: a perfect circle, drilled with precision, now revealing Ingrid's haunt. I waved to the maid who stood more frozen than her boss' face. So. Another "accident" that was not one. And it had nearly yielded not Chanel, but Body No. 5.

I wanted to print the room, though if I knew my man, he'd surely worn gloves. And footprints? The dummies at Mammoth had thought to vacuum—that day—based on the carpet's deep ridges. I sighed. Manly could cover up better than Gypsy Rose Lee. Though I searched for other clues, my effort was half-hearted. When you blipped off four people in public, you had to know your trade.

"Let's go," I said to Errol, leading him from the dark room to the overly generous sun. I reached into my bag for a pair of tinted cheaters.

"You look like a star!" Errol crowed, but I think he just wanted to cheer me. "So . . . nothing?"

"Nope." I led him back to the Ford now proudly boasting a ticket. One penned by lot security which I cheerfully tore in two. "Now we know for a fact these 'accidents' are hooey. As if Magee didn't confirm that."

I shuddered.

"What now?" asked Errol.

"Let's tell Lenski he needs to shell out for a guard. This last near-miss is the only time our hatchetman hasn't left a stiff, and I'll bet a dollar to a Canadian dime he's going to try again."

"Right."

We weren't far from Thalberg's white columns, so after being admitted to the sacred floor, we talked to Lenski's secretary.

"Ingrid Johansson," I told her without preliminaries. "Let Mr. Lenski know she needs round-the-clock security. And not one of these studio boobs—a real john or ex G-man."

Shaherzad nodded. I hoped she made a good salary. She deserved it, having to read aloud novels like *Gone with the Wind*. For those thousand-plus pages alone, she should get double golden time.

We went back to the Ford (no new ticket!), and I drove out the east gate. After the last two days, I needed something to lift my spirits.

"Hey, Errol," I said, "Lenski gave me more dough, so let's hit the counter at Schwab's. I've got a real craving for a very chocolatey shake."

"You don't have to twist my claw!" he yelled, nearly hitting his head on the roof. "Sunset or bust!"

Chapter 25
Ask an Expert

We emerged from Schwab's almost blotto from rich chocolate and richer whipped cream. I even slurped up the extra in its little tin cup.

"Whoo!" yelled Errol, doing a neat 360 on the sidewalk. If tourists thought a revolving dragon was anything to gawk at, they didn't. It was Hollywood, after all.

"Errol," I said, my head spinning though I stood in place, "I'm stuck. Even bursting with sugar, I don't know what to do next." I thought back to all the crime fiction I'd read at UCLA: *Maltese Falcon* and *The Big Sleep*. "What would Sam Spade do?" I asked.

"Why don't you ask him?" I was just about to tell Errol that Spade was uh, strictly fictional, but he cut me off. "I'm not a dumb bunny!" he cried. "I know what's real and what isn't. What I'm saying is this: Why not go to Musso and Frank's? I hear Chandler's a regular. At the bar, that is."

"Ah."

Even though Errol could drive me spare, he sure had his moments. *Why didn't I think of that?*

"Can I go in with you?" he asked.

I frowned, though based on rumors, the gallons of booze consumed at that bar might make him look perfectly normal. Besides, the grill was on Hollywood Boulevard: birthplace of general nuttiness.

"All right," I said, reaching to open the Ford. Soon, we were heading north on Sunset. "Just keep buttoned and let me talk."

"Yes, ma'am!" said Errol, saluting me with a claw.

I made a right on the boulevard. My old and current stomping ground. Fifteen minutes later, I pulled in front of the grill.

Musso & Frank's looked like it'd been here forever—who, knows, maybe it had been. Just like the swanky nightclubs, its stark white face hid the magic within.

Errol and I got out. He stopped before a window, smoothing down his spikes before slapping on his fedora.

"You look sharp," I told him. "Just be sure to *stay* sharp and say nothing."

He rolled his eyes before bending his way through the door.

"We're in!" he breathed as we strolled past the entrance.

And there *was* magic: not of the tinsel variety but of men and women whose books had defined this century. I'd heard Hemingway, Parker, F. Scott shot the breeze in its smoky bar. Speaking of Fitzgerald, I saw him in mid-conversation with, judging by his posture, another tipsy writer. I squinted at the bright lights hanging from venerable walls, each faux-leather booth festooned by a tall wooden spear. I had a feeling that stars like Ingrid and Carrie would rather die than walk in here.

Still, I wasn't them, and this joint was above my pay grade. I slipped into an empty chair not far from my quarry, Errol to my left.

"Scotch," I told the bartender. "No ice and no soda."

"I'll have the same," said Errol, moving his head to peer around me—at the two writers who seemed on the verge of a quarrel.

"Mr. Fitzgerald," I ventured after my drink had arrived. "I can't tell you how much I enjoyed *Gatsby*. I read it at UCLA, and I'll never forget it.

He stared at me through thick cheaters which remined me of Lenski's.

"Thank you, my dear," he bowed, now so drunk his arm tumbled his tumbler. "Not like *myself*, I'm afraid." He looked as sad as the boozehounds sleeping against the Proctor.

"Well," I asked, "why not write another novel?"

"Most people don't know I'm alive." His hand was visibly shaking. "Think I died with the 20's."

"Well, here you are!" I cried. "Seems like Hollywood's bad for you. Why not get out of town?"

"CAN'T," he said loudly, causing a few heads to turn. "Need the money. Movies pay a fortune."

"But Scott," said his friend, moving a booze-filled container out of Fitzgerald's grasp. "They don't like you. You get drunk and then you're fired."

Fitzgerald nodded, his expression that of a man confiding a huge secret.

"That's 'cause I'm *always* drunk," he said, but there was no regret, only a handsome grin. "Got to be. Only way to stomach the bosses."

After Lenski and Manly, I was inclined to agree. Maybe Fitzgerald was right: just stay blitzed all the time. I leaned back, addressing his friend.

"Excuse me," I said, not bothering to smile since he looked so grave. "Do you know if Raymond Chandler still frequents this place?"

"Who wants to know?" asked the man, placing a pipe in his mouth to light it.

"Nicky Forenza," I said, embarrassed to go on. "Private eye."

"Well." The man leaned back as we talked over Fitzgerald. "I'm him." He chuckled. "Might want to ask you some questions."

"That's why I'm here," I confessed. "To ask *you* some." I burbled nervously before the man whose books immortalized Bogie, relating the whole Mammoth saga without any names. I finished my story and my Scotch. Chandler just stared.

"Hmm," he said. "If I were you, I'd find a connection: between the stiffs, the girl, and the killer."

"I've tried!" I protested. "Even the head of the studio is completely in the dark."

Chandler let out a puff of white smoke.

"Hardly surprising. Those producers know nothing. So little they paired me up with a bore like 'Wild Billy'!"

Errol couldn't keep still. I knew he wouldn't.

"Mr. Chandler," he gasped, "for what it's worth, I think *Double Indemnity* is one of the greats!"

"My partner is a rabid fan of the pictures."

"And works in them too, I assume."

Not wanting to lie to my hero, I answered with a weak smile.

"Mr. Chandler, if you were Phillip Marlowe, what would *you* do?"

The writer looked deadpan.

"Marlowe does exactly what I tell him."

My posture sagged.

"Of course."

Another dead end.

"But." I perked up. "If I were a sleuth," he said, "I'd head over to Studio Legal."

"Find a lawyer?" I asked. Was Ingrid planning to sue me?

"Yes. They have records of all the credits—who worked on what and when. There might be a project which involved all of your victims. If you find it, study it carefully. There might be a buried clue." Fitzgerald hiccuped. "Well, seems it's time for Scott to retire. Nice talking to a real PI."

I wanted to pull an Errol and present a napkin for an autograph, then pulled up short. Christ, I was thirty-one, not twelve. I emerged with most of my dignity back on the sidewalk with Errol. He at least waited a minute before his "I told you so."

"See?" he asked, jabbing me in the ribs. "What'd I tell you? Chandler pulls Marlowe's strings, and they're both genius detectives!"

"Yeah, yeah," I mumbled, hating to be bested. "Let's hop back in the jalopy and get to Mammoth Legal. Maybe Chandler is right and there's some clue shut in a drawer."

"Can I come?" Errol asked. This refrain was getting more familiar than "Happy Birthday."

"Not this time," I said. "I might have to bat my lashes and I need to do it alone."

"Fine," he huffed, but I could tell he was hurt.

"Hey—why don't you go back to the office and listen to *Ellery Queen?* Maybe you'll pick up a tip."

"Right!" He was back to his old bouncing self. "If you don't come home by six, I'm getting Bill on the horn."

"I don't need a cop to protect me. That's up to Smith & Wesson."

I patted my bag.

Errol didn't look too sure.

Chapter 26

First We Kill All the Lawyers

After I dropped Errol off, I headed to Culver City, but the Ford started making strange sounds like she'd had enough of Mammoth. Frankly, so I had. I played it smart and came in by Thalberg where studio business seemed to be run. After my usual dance with the guard, I got a pass, a space, and directions. *I might as well,* I thought, *set myself up with an office.* For the present, I passed those white columns and headed for faceless buildings. Expecting Legal to be one of them, I started when I discovered its front was a lively set!

In pictures, it seemed, the stardust covered everyone.

I entered below a mockup of St. Louis to confront the usual receptionist: well-dressed, young, and blonde.

"I'm working for Mr. Lenski," I explained, flashing my pass.

"I can see that," she said, rolling her eyes. "Who is it you want to see?"

I felt like saying "Tarzan" but that would just provoke her.

"Someone in Legal, please."

She surveyed me before she picked up the phone.

"There's a woman here doing work for Mr. Lenski. Could you please send Mr. Goetz down?" She hung up. "He'll just be a minute."

That was it. No offer of coffee, water, or a seat. As promised, an elevator soon expelled a man in a somber suit.

"I'm Mr. Goetz," he told me. "And you are—?"

"Nicky Forenza. I'm handling an urgent matter for Mr. Lenski."

Goetz, thirtyish and not bad-looking, snapped to attention at the mention of his boss. He summoned me into the elevator, then turned.

"How can I help you, Mrs. Forenza?"

"Miss."

"Apologies."

He didn't look like he was sorry.

"Mr. Goetz, I wondered if I could have a look at credits dating back to the Silents."

"Doing research for Lenski's memoir?"

"No."

I stopped talking.

"Very well, er, let me show you the files. We have to clear every title card to make sure it's correct."

"Fascinating."

"I wouldn't know," he huffed, "we lawyers perform *important* work."

"Like suing everyone?" I asked.

He winced.

"I'll just leave you to it."

He walked off so fast he was a blur of brown. I shrugged. I wasn't here to make friends.

I started with a drawer marked "1920's"—the Silents. I vaguely remembered them and not too fondly. The melodrama grated on me and the actors were so "big" they could be playing on Broadway. Still,

Ma swooned over Valentino, and I had to admit that Doug Fairbanks was good with a sword. These thoughts sustained me as I pulled out one moldy yellow folder after another, scanning credits of marginal films with all the zeal of a sloth. 1921, 22, 23: all the names started to jumble, and I couldn't remember if Ingrid had starred in *The Shiek* or *The Temptress*. Then a light went off: not in the building (they had a union to deal with that) but in my fatigued mind.

Why not simply look up Ingrid's credits, I thought, then see which picture or pictures included the "silent" four victims. Reenergized, I found a bank of dull gray file cabinets captioned only by the typewritten card, "Stars." I jumped in like tabbing through yellowing papers was like winning an Oscar. Coming to the "J's," I found "Johannsson," and grabbed the thick file, seating myself at a small chair and table that reminded me of Hollywood Grammar.

I whipped out a blank paper and pen, taking notes when I saw a familiar name. I'd always been a good student, and it wasn't long before I had three titles before me listing joint credits for Felize, Alexander, Haskel and Magee. I focused hard on the list. Which could cough up a clue?

I knew what I needed: a film historian. With reluctance, I took the elevator downstairs, asking the wisegal receptionist directions to the studio Library.

"Egghead, huh?" she remarked. She'd ceased the important work of painting her nails. Jungle Red. Bored, she half-heartedly pointed the way, and I set out, prepared to meet my nemesis.

I hadn't forgotten the sneaky four-eyes who'd helped to out Errol. So, with caution, I stepped into a small, squat building to find inside not a library's strict order but a tumble of books. I faced yet another assistant. Christ, the gatekeepers on the lot all looked like eager bulldogs.

"Excuse me," I said, waving my list, "I wonder if I could consult the head librarian."

This bulldog, dark-haired and demure, opened her mouth to protest. "I really need a film expert," I cooed, "to answer a difficult question."

"Ooh," she said, going from cold to warm like an electric blanket. "I'll get Mr. Kenyon."

"Thanks."

While she went in the back, I looked over the tall books strewn across the counter: on everything from the Old South to the Battle of Britain. Most were heavily illustrated.

"Yes?"

Just as I'd pictured him, Kenyon limped up to me, his gray stubble giving him the look of the drunks I used to haul in the tank. He wore an old yellow sweater, no tie, and a pair of heavy glasses too tired to perch on his nose.

"Mr. Kenyon, could you please look these three titles over and tell me—is there anything special about any of them?"

"'Special?'" he asked, throwing me a look of disdain. "Every producer thinks their film is spec—" He squinted over my list. "These two were 'B's,'" he mumbled, "throwaway stuff. But this one . . ." He pointed a shaky finger. "This one's kind of a legend."

"Oh?" I tried to keep my breath steady.

"Yeah, *The Iron Horse.* Supposed to be some kind of masterpiece, but the negative and all the prints are lost."

"You mean . . . there's no trace of it?"

"That's right, little lady. Most negatives here were melted down for silver. And silent prints are God knows where."

The studios, I thought sarcastically, *really treasure their output.* Once a movie was shown, it was promptly thrown in the trash.

"Mr. Kenyon, you've been extremely valuable—"

"Usually am." His voice popped like a bad soundtrack. "Now, if you'll excuse me, I have to get back to the Caribbean."

I half-expected him to swing out a suitcase but he just limped behind his stacks.

Strange guy, I thought, *but this might be my first real clue.*

Chapter 27
The Yachting Life

I couldn't wait to get back to Errol. I stopped the wheezing Ford by a phone booth, then called the office.

"Errol," I panted, "I think I have something."

"Great! What is it?"

"The Iron Horse."

"Sounds familiar." As he thought, the line buzzed with static. "Wait! That's McSweeney's lost picture!"

"So you've heard of it."

"Sure. Can you imagine how cheesed off he must be?"

I didn't really care about the director's mood.

"We've got to tail him. Before he kills again."

"Madame Peeper," said Errol, "you're putting the cart before the iron horse. I admit he's the Number One Suspect. But to call him a murderer—"

"Okay, Okay," I said hastily, "'alleged.' In any case, we have to find him."

"Look no further than Catherine Wescott."

"The actress?"

"And two-time Oscar winner. Scuttlebutt is . . ." he lowered his voice. "She and McSweeney are 'involved.'"

"So?"

"He's married, and his wife is so Catholic she makes the Pope look like a rabbi."

"Oh boy."

"You said it."

Errol's voice cracked across the line.

"According to *Movie Life*, Westcott's a frequent guest on his yacht, *The Shamrock*."

"Great name," I quipped, before hearing the phone click off.

Damn. That was my last nickel.

Still, I parked the Ford illegally and trundled up to the office. There, I saw Errol, his snout hidden behind some glossy rag. When he saw me, he leapt up and bounced.

"Well?" I asked.

"I found it! *The Shamrock* sails from Long Beach, and when McSweeney's not shooting, he takes her out every weekend."

"The wife go with him?"

"Ha! Not with Wescott in a cabin!"

"Tomorrow's Saturday," I said, staring at the hanging wall calendar with its adorable kittens. The bank had given them out for free. "We need to get ourselves there. Stow away and watch. McSweeney might have a loose tongue."

"He's a hell of a drinker," said Errol. "Makes Fitzgerald look like Jean Nation."

"I'm liking this plan," I said. "Just have to find a way to Long Beach on a machine that can make it."

"Bill?" he asked.

"Nah. I don't want him in this mess. The Chief'll want to put the bite on someone."

"Our men in blue," cracked Errol.

The next morning, I pilfered through my small wardrobe, finally finding a summery blouse and white trousers which I matched with tan-and-white Oxfords. Wescott would be proud.

Once I'd tossed its ticket, I drove the old Ford to Normandie to hop on the Red Car. Once Errol boarded, he did get a few strange looks from "nonpros" (or those *not* in the Industry, I'd been told). Once we sat down, I was sure to talk loudly about his upcoming picture, *Dragons Take the West.* The passengers relaxed visibly, ignoring us "show biz folks." We chugged along the tracks that might have inspired *The Iron Horse,* and I knew for a fact Mammoth used the red car to shlep to Valley premieres.

May it stay in the city forever! I thought, watching Hollywood recede as downtown came into view. At Union Station (my old haunt!), we had to get off to board the Southern Line. After waiting a few, we were off again, now passing through some not-so-great parts of L.A.: Compton, Dominguez, Del Amo. The depressing industrial landscape continued into Long Beach, which I knew from working at Lockheed housed a huge Navy shipyard.

Once Errol and I got off, we found ourselves close to the water, and walked a couple rough blocks past shipbuilding types. I must have looked like I had the bees in my ridiculous outfit: just another rich girl straight out of the pages of *Gatsby*. Once we got to the dock, and the not-great smell of the sea, I turned to Errol.

"So," I said, "any clue where this *Shamrock* is berthed?"

"Look for a huge wooden ship," he said, "with rigging enough for four sails."

"How about just the name?" I asked, pointing to a white ship with "Shamrock" painted on its bow.

"Oh," he said, his scaled cheeks tinging light red.

"Follow me," I said, on the lookout for errant crewmen.

How did you, I wondered, *sneak aboard a hundred-foot private yacht?*

Look like you belonged there, I decided.

I saw a gangplank propped at her side like in some old pirate picture, and motioned to Errol. There were crewmen aboard—in *uniform*, no less!—but they seemed more interested in unfurling sails and making sure that the deck was Hollywood clean. With Errol pushing my back, we arrived onboard by the stern, where I quickly pushed open a door and shuttled us into a cabin.

"Not bad." I looked around, seeing décor that must have come from a set designer. It was homey—with shamrock-patterned curtains and lots of green, a nod to the Old Country—with a fully-stocked bar and bed big enough for two. I wondered how often that mattress got a workout.

"Nicky—" Errol began.

"Shhh!" I cautioned. No point in being caught before we'd hit the waves.

We waited. And waited. I helped myself to a Bacardi while Errol peeped out the porthole.

Finally, we heard voices, mainly male and mainly loud. I joined Errol to see the captain—dressed for the part—a very big guy I knew was Robert Marion, the Western star; a couple of guys I didn't recognize, and—Catherine Wescott, her outfit like mine but much more expensive.

More yelling, and we got underway, sailing away from Long Beach and toward God-knows-where. We'd have to be able to eavesdrop to make this trip worthwhile. So, I motioned Errol out the cabin, looking for a way to climb up. But he just shook his head, leading me to a large tube polished to perfection.

"Speaking tube," he whispered. "I saw it in *First Comes Cowardice.*" *Strange title,* I thought, *but just now, it wasn't worth a hill of beans.*

Errol and I crowded around the curved tube, putting our ears as close as possible. I never knew dragons had such sharp hearing until he started whispering.

"They're calling some guy 'The Admiral,' and I think it's McSweeney," he said.

"Sickening," I mumbled.

"Well," said Errol, "now he's telling war stories about when his ship was part of the Navy and he was made a Captain."

I snorted.

"What'd he do? Film things?"

Errol bent forward, listening.

"You're right on the money. That's *exactly* what he did."

"Bet he was right there at Normandy."

Errol listened again.

"Sounds like he was. And he was wounded at Midway."

"Run out of 35MM?" I quipped.

There wasn't much after that. I glanced out a nearby porthole and saw the Pacific's cold waves. Speaking of which, one of nausea swept over me, but I fought it like Pops would.

Errol and I lounged by the tube, listening as loud voices got louder—and quite a bit merrier. Liquid joy was imbibed up above, and there was even singing—hideously offkey.

"Great," I huffed, "just our luck to get on the booze cruise."

"Maybe McSweeney'll say something he shouldn't."

"He better, before we end up in Mexico."

After about an hour, the voices above faded: maybe those wild partiers had folded and were catching some Z's. That's when a hull door opened, leading Errol and I to scramble behind some ropes. What we saw was McSweeney—in full Navy regalia—and Wescott, looking regal even as she slutted around. They both crept drunkenly toward the cabin we had vacated, then slammed the door behind them, accompanied by throaty laughs.

What would the Pope think? I wondered.

Despite my better judgment, I put my ear to the door. What I heard from Wescott was not the perfect, upper-class diction she reserved for the screen.

"Errol, I don't think this is going to work. We're stuck on this crate forever."

"Or until they finish," he added.

"I hope so. Or I'm going to swab this deck with my breakfast."

"Whoa," said Errol, sliding as far away as he could.

When Wescott and her paramour finally emerged, seeming a tad more sober, I breathed a sigh of relief. *Could we go back to port now?* Surely, these busy Hollywood folks couldn't take the time for a Mexican cruise.

Thank the Saints, I was right! I felt the ship pivot, then do a complete 180. We were cutting through waves toward Long Beach! At this point, I didn't care if a U-Boat started firing, as long as we made it home!

We made it. But I was in bad shape. Errol, of course, was fine, wagging his spade tail as we disembarked after McSweeney and his guests. It was now or never.

I swaggered up to the director, who wore dark glasses despite the overhung sky.

"Mr. McSweeney," I told him. "I'm your biggest fan!"

His grim face almost smiled, but still held its semi-frown.

"Which one of mine is your favorite?"

"Oh, *How Green Was My Valley!*" called Errol. "And *The Informer* and *Grapes of Wrath*."

"How about *Stagecoach?*" asked Marion.

"Oh, Mr. Marion, you set the screen on fire!"

"I did not, didn't I?" he asked in his laconic drawl.

He turned with the others to go.

"My favorite's *The Iron Horse!*" I shouted. "How could they lose such a masterpiece! Mr. McSweeney, you must be so cheesed off!"

Now the director smiled.

"Nah," he said, waving dismissively. "Who the hell cares? It's just another picture."

Chapter 28
Seasick

The ride back on two red cars had all the joy of a funeral. Errol and I sat silent until we reached my joint. There, in my "bachelor" bathroom, I finally lost my breakfast.

"Not good," said Errol, shaking his head to go out. He came back shortly with a bag from Alpha Beta: one containing a carton of crackers and a bottle of ginger ale. "This is what the stars use after a night on the town," he told me.

Grateful, I took both his offerings, forcing them down. Even a saltine tasted like salted death.

"You should have said you get seasick," he scolded, flopping beside me on the couch.

"Not so hard," I said in a choked whisper. "And when would *I* have been on a boat? Do I look like a WAVE?"

"Nope, but a bunch sure tossed you and *you* tossed your—!"

"Can the vulgar humor." I wondered what Ma would say. "We did learn something, but we could've learned it onshore. McSweeney doesn't give a rat's ass for his silent 'masterpiece.'

So much for him as a suspect. The only things he's done wrong are stepping out on his wife and playing at being an Admiral."

"Well, sighed Errol, "at least it was a nice trip. Did you know Foreign Correspondent was shot in Lo—"

"Errol," I groaned, "please don't talk your arm off. I need quiet. And, um, quiet. Why don't you have a saltine?"

He seized the carton, upending crackers into his mouth.

Why did I have to put up with him, besides the promise of twenty-five grand? This got me to thinking—my head still worked even if my stomach didn't. There was something about Hughley's will that didn't make sense to me. It's almost like the tycoon *knew* he was going to die. Why else leave me the egg when he'd clearly put himself out to retrieve it? Going to the center of the Earth wasn't your everyday journey. He must have spent a lot of dough, which he had; but also time, which he didn't, considering his plane designs for the Air Force and his terrible motion pictures. Even a billionaire wanted to be a producer. I tried not to think of the ocean as I watched Errol finish the cartoon, then polish it off with the bottle he'd bought for *me*.

That egg must have meant something to Hughley, and by all the logic I knew, he should have wanted to keep it. But no—he'd willed it to me. To make sure the hatchling inside got a square break.

"Errol," I mumbled, seizing the bottle from his claw. "Tomorrow, we visit the Hall of Public Records."

Chapter 29
Next, Kill All the Lawyers

I knew downtown like the back of my hand, so once I'd concluded my stomach was no longer at sea, I grabbed the "N" with Errol, walking down to LAPD headquarters: the soaring white City Hall. This made me think of Bill, and I smiled.

Now, though, we marched toward the ancient L.A. Hall of Records, maybe not an eyesore when it was built in the tweens, but certainly a big one now. There were more oddly shaped windows than in a federal pen. In the lobby, a blue uniformed cop stopped us.

"Good morning," I said, "I'm here to consult Public Records."

"Let's see some ID," he demanded, jutting out his jaw.

"You see, that's what's so wonderful. Public records are public, and *anyone* can access them!"

"Smart-mouthed broad," I heard him mumble. "I'll be keeping my eye on you."

And Los Angeles, I thought, *should be keeping an eye on the whole of the LAPD.* With one notable exception.

"C'mon, Errol," I whispered.

"Hey," said the cop. "It ain't Halloween no more,"

"And more's the pity," I said, "but my friend here works for the movies." I bent and whispered. "He's one of those Method Actors—always in character."

"Swell," said the cop, clearly tired of all this screwiness.

After consulting a board, we took the elevator up, stepping off at Public Records. I had no idea how this worked—after all, I'd been a nursemaid and not a real cop. I stepped up to the counter, where a girl, not as officious as those at the studio, gave me a bleary-eyed glance.

"Hello," I said. "I'm interested in seeing Mr. Hugh Hughley's will."

"You and what army?" she crackled. "I've had ten birds this week trying to see if he left 'em sumthin'. Here."

She shoved over the unfiled document—as thick as I remembered. Miss L.A. gave Errol a look but didn't bother to comment. It might have taken too much of her energy. Errol and I took a place at another school-sized table.

"Remember this?" I asked him. He gave me a blank stare. "Oh. Sorry. You were just a blue egg." He shook his head as if searching for the nearest looney bin. "Okay." I separated the sheaf so he could go over half. I saw so much about Hughley's business: this plane went here; that airport went there—that I stifled a wide yawn.

"A good detective," Errol intoned, "never overlooks a detail."

"Where'd you pick that up? *Ellery Queen?*"

He squirmed. I was right.

I skimmed most of Hughley Industries, starting to pay attention when I got to the sensitive stuff. Goldstein hadn't been kidding! Most of Hughley's fortune had gone to his Mormon handlers. And his personal shyster got only five-thousand, and that to be measured out each quarter. What was Howie's sin, besides not being Mormon? Or had he done Hughley a nasty, and this was his boss' revenge?

I sat there quietly while Errol took down some notes. It wasn't exactly easy—not with nails the size of a toothbrush. Yet, he was moving along while I had come to a standstill.

What did I know about Goldstein? He'd made the papers occasionally, squiring his wife at this or that hoity-toity function. Then there'd been a shot of him and Hughley, standing before a blurred airfield.

Hmmm, I wondered, *hadn't that picture been recent? Like, right before Hughley's death?*

"Errol, we need the *Times*."

"I thought Lenski wanted to keep this out of the papers."

"He does. I just want to look at a clipping."

Lucky me, the *Times* building wasn't too far. A couple long blocks down 1st, and we were there. In the lobby, I finally had the chance to do something I hadn't done in awhile: I flashed my PI's license.

"Nicky Forenza," I told the harried girl. "Like to sneak a peek at your archives."

"Third floor," she yelled, picking up two ringing phones. I hoped she made more than fifty cents a week.

Another elevator. Another musty cavern filled with moldering paper. I checked the stacks, each month filed separately on a long, hanging rack. I went back a couple of weeks. It wasn't hard to find the article: Hughley's death, after all, had been the talk of the nation.

"Good," I told Errol, replacing yesterday's news. "We're off to Culver City."

"Not the red car again?" he groaned.

"I thought you liked it. Besides, this is important."

Back to Union Station, on the Western line this time. We got off at Culver City—home of Mammoth—but that wasn't my destination. No, instead I led Errol toward Jefferson, stopping at an enormous airfield.

"Hughley Private Airport" it read. In the middle I saw a runway so long it seemed to run the length of L.A.

"Uh, Nicky," Errol began, "what are we doing here?"

"Going in search of what Hollywood calls "the little people.""

"Couldn't we find them at Mammoth?"

"No."

We caught a ride on what looked like a golf cart up to one of several enormous hangars.

"Thanks," I told our driver. This was good luck. If you took more than one passenger on one of these carts at the studio, you had to call Transportation. Most of the hangars were shut tight, but one enormous door stood open. I nodded to Errol and we stepped inside. It was just like Lockheed, with helmeted workers scurrying around the floor, but there was a major difference: Hughley seemed to be building more parts than planes. This wasn't a total surprise: thanks to the ubiquitous *Times,* I'd read the aviator had built some planes for the war, but most turned out to be failures. From the looks of it, his company served as more of a parts warehouse than a manufacturer of aircraft.

I flashed my license again: to a young, ginger-haired kid. He still seemed wide-eyed, like I'd first been at Lockheed. He'd get over it. I shouted over the din of welders and engines being tested.

"HI. I'M WONDERING IF ANYONE HERE WAS THERE WHEN UH . . . MR. HUGHLEY CRASHED."

"WHICH TIME?" he yelled.

"THE LAST ONE," I shrugged.

"Yeah, I think so. Wait outside."

I couldn't be happier to be out of that noise factory. Two years of welding Lightnings had made my hearing less sharp. (Like the rest of me?)

Peering into the hangar, I saw the ginger pointing an old-timer our way. The grizzled worker in overalls looked at Errol without expression.

"Pictures," I said. That seemed to be enough.

"How kin I help you?" he asked, wiping grease from his forearm. How many men like this had I known, doing their all for the war at home while the boys fought overseas?

"You-you witnessed Mr. Hughley's last flight, Mister—?"

"Payne. Call me Owen. Yes, ma'am, I'm afraid I did."

"What kind of plane was he flying?"

"One he'd designed—the XF-11."

"I heard about those," I said. "The guys at Lockheed said it was a like a bigger Lightning."

"Just so," said Owen, nodding. "Mr. Hughley was the first to fly her."

"And the last?" I asked dispassionately.

Owen sighed.

"'Fraid so. He crashed right in Beverly Hills—took out two houses."

"And himself."

"It's a huge loss. Mr. Hughley was a one-off."

"So I've heard," I said diplomatically. "Did he generally pilot his own test planes?"

"Oh, yes, ma'am. He wouldn't let nobody near 'em until he gave 'em a whirl."

"Did you see the actual crash?" asked Errol.

I suppressed a grin. He'd make a shamus yet.

"Oh no. I was right here, on the airfield. Did see the takeoff, though."

"And it seemed smooth?"

"Like black-market nylons."

"Hmmm." I thought. "Did you or Mr. Hughley or anyone else suspect the plane would crash?"

"We try not to think of those things. Bad luck."

"Of course." I directed my eyes to Owen's. There was something in them—something he wasn't saying. "Can you tell me anything else about the crash? Any suspicions of foul play?"

There it was in his eyes—an angry blaze like a falling star.

"I-I shouldn't . . ."

"You admired Mr. Hughley, you said. Who here would want him dead?"

"Not-not here," Owen mumbled.

That's when I struck like a twenty-foot shark-in-waiting.

"Are you acquainted with Howard Goldstein, Mr. Hughley's lawyer?"

Owen snorted.

"He's too high and mighty to speak to the likes of me!"

"But you've seen him?" I asked.

"Sure. Used to stay so close to the boss, I thought he had patio furniture set up in his—"

"Owen. When was the last time you saw Goldstein?"

He bowed his head and sighed.

"On that day."

"The day Hughley crashed?"

He nodded.

"What was he doing here? Was he some kind of aircraft fan?"

"Ha! Prob'ly wanted to see if his personal bank survived."

"And when it didn't?"

Owen scratched his chin.

"I may be wrong, but he didn't seem sad. He sure left in a hurry though."

"Do you know where he was going?"

"No ma'am. Just got into a Rolls and blew."

"Thank you, Owen. You've been very helpful."

I crumpled a C-note into his palm.

"Oh! No need for that." Still, he took it. He looked down. "I really liked Mr. Hughley. He could be screwy, but he was a true airman."

"His name will live on." I smiled as he turned back to the hangar, ready to resume work. Then I walked back toward the runway with Errol. "What do you make of all that?" I asked.

"It's a lot to swallow. Hughley seemed decent enough—I mean, he did care about *me*—" He winked. "But all the dope on Goldstein: What was his angle?"

"That's what I'm wondering. He'd drafted his boss' will—knew Hughley only left him five grand. Why then, kick up his heels when his client's plane crashed?"

We exchanged a hard glance as we made our way back to the red car stop.

"Insurance," we both said, remembering Mrs. Felize.

Chapter 30
A Kindred Soul

I'd never been a desk jockey, and I have to admit my feeling sorry for them was mixed with a fair bit of hate. That's what I tried to damp down as Errol and I swung into yet another faceless building. This time, in Culver City.

"Yes?" the half-dead receptionist asked. She had all the zip of a mummy.

I flashed the well-used license.

"Nicky Forenza, PI. I'm investigating the Hughley case."

"Oh." Her eyes remained dead. "Then you'll have to see Mr. Keyes. He's in charge of that policy."

"Thanks, doll," said Errol, but even his scaly charm couldn't rouse a flicker of life. She pointed us toward a desk in a jumble of them.

"Mr. Keyes?" I asked, surveying the older man hunched over his work. He looked like he'd seen his share of fraud. After brief introductions, I got right to the point. "Would it be possible to see any insurance policies taken out on Hugh Hughley? The more recent, the better."

Keyes sat back in his ill-fitting suit. Guess they didn't pay him enough.

"Well . . ." he looked me over, his gaze settling on Errol.

"Pictures," I said.

He nodded.

"Mrs. Forenza—"

"Miss."

"Apologies. Miss Forenza, you and I are in the same business. We both fox around trying to sniff out a crime." He rolled back his chair, opening up his bottom desk drawer. "These came in a few weeks ago. Most are ringers."

He shoved some papers toward me. I quickly leafed through them: most were laughable, claiming Hughley had promised them insurance money. Sure. And I was Heddy Lamar. The last one caught my eye: it was neat and signed by Goldstein. So. Howie had gotten his revenge on the Mormons, after all, giving himself five mil in case of his boss' demise. I had no doubt he'd fixed that "crash"—maybe with another mechanic. I wanted to nail him then, but decided to wait in case he was mixed up with Mammoth.

"Thanks, Mr. Keyes," I smiled. "Mind if I make a copy?"

He got up—painfully—and approached a mimeograph. After a few minutes, he returned with what I'd asked for. Boy, did it smell! I shook the investigator's hand before landing outside with Errol. I tried to make sense of this latest angle.

"So," I said as we entered a drugstore for coffee. We were so close to Mammoth the guy behind the counter just gave Errol a wink.

"Yeah?"

Errol picked up his cup with both hands and drained it.

"Let's try to put this together," I said. "Felize wasn't the first victim: That honor goes to Hughley."

Errol shook his head.

"Set up by his own lawyer."

"And that surprises you why?" I took a bitter sip. "The question is: does Hughley's murder fit with the others? I mean, he was a 'film producer'—"

"Right," said Errol. "He always starred Roz Robust, that dame with the huge mel—"

"That isn't important," I snapped. "Just that he was in the Business. Did the killer make some connection between Hughley and the others."

"Don't forget Johansson."

I thought of her face.

"That would be tough."

"You know . . . Hughley had an affair with her after he broke up with Wescott. I read it in *Screen Romance.*"

Except this happened *offscreen.* I shook my head. Had *everyone* in this town slept with everyone else?

"How did it end?"

"Well . . . rumor has it she fancies the ladies. And is making out with Freida Braun."

"The German?"

"She's jake. Hitler hates her. And when Hughley found out about Freida, he dumped her. He's from the Midwest, conservative."

"What the hell was he doing in Hollywood?" I motioned for more coffee. "Good to know." I brooded over my brew. "I'm not sure what to do next. I could get Lenski to force Johansson to talk to us, but I think it's best if we see her in her native habitat."

"The set?" Errol asked, sipping his second cup slowly.

"More like a club. Someplace she's relaxed, and we can ask about Hughley."

"You think she conspired with Goldstein?"

"There's a chance. Spurned lover, and all that." I glanced down at the gleaming white counter. "I suppose you know where she goes?"

"Sure. The Grove. I've seen pictures in *Movie Life*."

"The what?"

"Cocoanut. Top glam spot forever."

I stared into my cup and groaned. I knew what this meant.

"Not the dress—again?"

Erroll motioned to a payphone in the corner.

"Better call Bill," he said.

Chapter 31
Swingin' at the Grove

Bill was so glad to hear from me his voice broke once or twice. I was determined to make it up to him: the cold shoulder after Mocambo's.

This time, I vowed, *I'd be as warm as the Grove's tropic décor.*

Errol had filled me in, and by the time he got back from the cleaners, it was nearly time to go. Though I wasn't a big boozer, I took a swig of Bacardi: for fortification, I told myself. This time, Errol helped me into The Dress: we'd spent so much time together since he'd cracked open that egg, I no longer felt shy for him to see me in my underthings. Though he'd muttered something like, "Nice jugs!" I let him get away with it. I was too nervous about tonight.

"Suppose I can't come?" he sighed once I'd been poured into gold beads.

"Sorry," I said. "When it plays, I think Hollywood wants to forget the Business."

He nodded reluctantly.

"I'll be at the office."

I grabbed my Adrian bag.

"Why?"

He gave me a scaly smile.

"Just in case," he said, "you want to bring Bill up for a nightcap."

Damn! I blushed, and he noticed.

"Good luck, dollface," he winked. "On all fronts."

I heard a horn from below and squeezed myself into the elevator. The telephone girl downstairs didn't give me a second look.

"Nik!" Bill called when he saw me. "You look gorgeous as usual."

"Three time's a charm," I cracked, making sure to lean over and kiss him on his cheek. "What're you driving this time?" He grinned, taken aback by my gesture, then secured his arm above my waist—to touch my gaps of exposed flesh—and led me to an open-topped black Benz waiting at the curb. "They just get better and better!" I laughed.

He leaned in while opening my door.

"So do you," he whispered. I waited for a kiss, but none came. Before this night was over, I determined to find a fix. "How's my lady detective?" he asked, whipping his head toward me.

"Puzzled," I said. "I think I've stumbled on another murder."

"Who is it this time?" he asked. "The makeup man?"

"A bit higher on the food chain. This one was a producer."

"Lenski won't stand for that!"

"This bird didn't work for Mammoth. He's got his own studio."

"Hope it wasn't Selznick!" Bill cried, "though that would have made the papers."

"Oh, our man did. But it had nothing to do with pictures."

"Hmmm. Since you can't tell me more, I'll just have to imagine."

I gave my best imitation of Jean—a half sultry smile.

"You do that," I purred.

Was I giving out enough hints?

This drive was longer than the ones we'd taken before: we went south down Hollywood, passing the major streets: Sunset, Santa Monica. I was glad. The Strip had become too familiar. I enjoyed a hint of L.A. wind as Bill turned right on Wilshire, turning opposite the Brown Derby. Too bad it wasn't still shaped like a hat.

"We're here," Bill crowed, sliding aside for the valet.

I looked up. We'd arrived at the Ambassador Hotel, set off from Wilshire and looking more like an army compound. I raised my brows.

"Moving fast, aren't we?" I cooed.

"Oh, Nicky!" Bill laughed, putting a dark-suited arm around me. "The Cocoanut Grove is inside!"

My second blush of the night. I'd have to stop doing this. Bill asked the valet for directions to the club, and put his arm in mine as he approached a long white awning with "Cocoanut Grove" emblazoned in black frilly letters. My third club in two weeks. At this rate, I'd make the *Times* "Society" pages!

Even though Errol had filled me in, I wasn't prepared for the Grove's décor: a kind of cross between Trader Vic's and a local luau. Were those actually *rubber palm trees* shading the tables from every wall? And was the ceiling really carved, Alladin-like, into a Moorish dome? I didn't have time to consider, since an older waiter practically flew us to a table. I looked around. Despite my disdain for the Industry, I wasn't dead. I recognized Brock Powell, the dark-haired King of Hollywood; Syd Chartreuse, the dancing dynamo; and even those I'd met: like Lenski, shaking his tush on the dance floor with some incomparable starlet; and Ingrid, huddled in a corner with the sultry Freida Braun.

Surrounded by "more stars than there were in Heaven," I felt every inch the "nonpro," even in Jean's gold dress. Bill seemed to pick up on my nerves, since he ordered us both a stiff bourbon.

"I suppose this is the ultimate," I said, watching couples swing to the orchestra on the bandstand.

"The Oscars are held here—did you know?" he asked.

"Why no. They could be held in my bathtub and I wouldn't notice."

As our tumblers arrived, he laughed.

"At least our drinks don't have little palms in them."

"Yes, we should be grateful."

This time, I wanted for us to eat dinner without being interrupted: by Hollywood players or my thoughts. So I felt determined to enjoy my Melon Cocktail (in honor of Errol), Broiled Salmon with Anchovy Butter, and a glorious dessert of Strawberry Cream Pie. Now, I was ready to confront the enemy, but first, I wanted to try something.

"Bill—you know, we've never danced at one of these things. There's always a Mrs. Felize or Meir Lenski hellbent on bothering us."

"Well, this is a wrong that must be righted!" He stood up, coming around to my chair to help me up. "Shall we?"

Happily, the band was playing a waltz and not a tropical rhumba. I folded myself into Bill's arms, happy not to ruin the neighborhood of these Industry glitterati. Most of all, I was happy just to be held by Bill, to feel his strong arms around me, one holding my hand and the other around my waist. I started to think that Ma's idea of me finding a man might not be so goofy.

We sailed under palms, and I could almost imagine myself on some white-sand beach. But the illusion was broken as we one-two-threed past Ingrid, and—as always—duty called. I halted before her and the glamorous Frieda Braun. At their side stood a commanding figure.

"Miss Johansson," I said, "forgive me, but we've met before."

"Ah jas," she drawled, "you ahre the dick."

Even if I hadn't known, her singsong speech instantly pegged her as Swedish.

"Private," I added. I bowed my head to her companion. "Miss Braun," I said. "I hope you're faring well in spite of the war."

"Ja," she answered, her beauty so sharp and cold I felt she could cut me. "You Ah-mericans are vonderful—ahnd I star in zo many wahr films."

Right, I thought. *This one's bright and no pushover.*

"Hello," I said to the gentleman, who ignored me with impunity. His posture was ramrod-straight, as if he'd been in the service, and a single black monocle covered one light eye. He could have been in the movies.

"Fasziniert," he drawled.

Wasn't anyone in this joint from the good old USA?

"This is Heinrich von Heinrich," said Ingrid. "He directed me in the Silents."

"And I vould still, if only zeh'd let me!"

His German accent made Freida's sound like she was from the Valley. Eyeing me from stem to stern, he marched over to take my hand and kiss the back of it.

"Charmed," I said, though I wasn't. "Miss Johannson," I ventured, digging my heels into the floor. "I had some dealings with poor Mr. Hughley. I understand he, uh . . . moved on before his unfortunate death."

Ingrid shrugged, giving Freida a look.

"I do miss him," said the Swede, "but we did remain friends. We stayed on the best of terms. Until . . . the end."

"A shame," said von Heinrich, "that isn't true of *all* your old friends."

Ingrid remained stone-faced. She wasn't called "The Sphinx" for nothing. But something in her voice convinced me she did miss Hughley.

"I'm sorry.," I said. "I mean—that he's gone."

"Not to vorry!" chirped Frieda, lighting a cigarette on a slim holder. "I'll keep her mind off men!"

Giving a naughty wink, she dragged Ingrid onto the dance floor. With her perfect legs and figure, Frieda could prove quite a distraction.

"If you'll excuse me."

Von Heinrich bowed stiffly, making his way to a sambaing Lenski. That man could move his hips. But from his sour expression, I could see he was less than thrilled.

"Well," I murmured to Bill, as we now rhumbaed past Lenski. The studio head was far better at it than I was. "I think that removes Ingrid from my list of suspects. It's not like she hates Hughley for throwing her over."

"Maybe she's done better," Bill grinned.

"Maybe," I agreed, thinking of the German bombshell. "Well," I said with regret, "I guess my foxing here is over."

"But not the night," he reminded, and we danced until two, even outlasting Lenski!

I was tired but exhilarated on our drive home. Now I wrapped myself in the mink since at this time, even L.A. could get chilly. I saw bars and clubs spilling out happy patrons, and I started to think that L.A.—and not New York—was the town that never sleeps. In any case, when Bill swung me into the lobby, we were alone: Miss Telephone had retired.

"So," I said, channeling Jean like a spirit. "Want to come up for coffee?"

He shrugged.

"Why not?"

We were silent in the elevator and when I opened my door. I sighed. He'd never seen my joint and it wasn't exactly a mansion perched on Sunset.

"Cozy," he remarked, ever the gentleman.

"That's one way to put it." I started into the "kitchen." Coffee or Bacardi?"

"Just a cup. I had enough to drink tonight."

"Me too." I'd actually taken it easy but booziness always loves company.

I scooped some dark grounds into the filter of my percolator, waiting for that "brewed" light like a wallflower at a dance. Wincing at my chipped mugs, I handed him one, then flopped down (as best I could in The Dress) next to him on the couch. He accepted the cup, taking a thoughtful sip.

"Oh!" I cried, "I forgot to ask if you take sugar or milk."

"I'm a cop," he smiled, "and strong joe is what makes us run."

"I wouldn't know," I sighed, thinking of my own fake Force days.

"You did fine," Bill told me, snaking his arm around my back. "As much as you could, in those days."

"Yeah." In other words: As much as a woman was *allowed* to do. I shook off my anger as Bill put down his cup.

This is it, I thought.

"Well, thanks for the coffee. I really should be going."

He made an effort to rise.

"NO!" My outburst surprised even me. "I mean—what's your hurry? Got an early shift?"

"As a matter of fact, I do."

He leaned in to peck me on my rouged cheek.

Was I really that beastly? I wondered. *Was a dame in a man's profession just a really big wet blanket?*

One thing you can say about it is, I've never lacked courage. Not in fighting Pops over UCLA, Ma and her Italian boys, and all of Mammoth in trying to solve its murders. I refused to turn yellow now.

Maybe my approach came off a bit strong, but I grabbed him around his head and smacked him one on the lips. Instead of retreating, he answered me with more pressure, tracing my hair with his fingers and ruining my curls, but I can't say that I cared.

"Nicky," he breathed, "I've wanted you for so long."

"So do something about it!" I said, taking a small breather.

He moved his hands above my waist, caressing the flesh of my sides. And the rest, you better believe, will end in a lingering FADE OUT.

Chapter 32
Howie Comes Clean

The next morning, I woke up in a pretty good mood. Even the sight of a boozer sprawled against my building didn't dampen my spirits. Errol swung in with a bag of pastries from Greenblatt's. I was touched, though he did use my dough.

"'Morning!" he chirped like Mellie in *Gone With the Wind*. Yes, I'd seen it. He threw down his twined box. "Well?"

"Well what?" I said coyly. Even though we were partners, I didn't have to tell him *everything*.

He stomped on one large foot.

"Bill! How'd it go?"

"Fine."

"That's it?!"

"That's all you're going to know."

"Don't you see," he asked, unwrapping a cherry Danish, "there are no lady dragons for me? That's why I have to live through you—so spill!"

I rolled my eyes, plugging in the percolator. I hated bottom-of-the-pot, but I hated waiting more.

"Look, Errol," I said, "let's just say that things . . . progressed. Will that keep your flames at bay?"

"Not really," he sighed, his mouth now lined in red fruit, "but I guess it'll have to do."

"You bet it will."

Errol sat down on a chair barely wide enough to contain him.

"So. Find out anything from Sweden?"

"Only that she's not sore at Hughley and says they parted friends. Speaking of which, I don't much like *hers.*"

"Oh?"

"They all seem to be German. Raises my hackles."

"Hey, you don't even have them!" He settled down. "Think they're collaborators?"

"I don't want to. That's how my Pops got nailed—and I know how rotten it is."

"What then?"

"Well, they seemed sleazy—like they were headed to an opium den. They remind me of what went on in Berlin—*before* the war."

Errol rose to fetch us two cups.

"Lots of show folk are sleazy—*especially* in this town. Did you hear Irv Strictly, head of Mammoth Publicity, had to whitewash Brock Powell's past? Seems he went from the oilfields to turning tricks on Santa Monica."

I hadn't known that, but I knew what went on on that street.

"Guess that doesn't make him a killer. Or all the others, either. I just feel . . . I'm missing something. Some piece that'll make the puzzle complete."

"I hope it's not of Switzerland. All the pieces are white."

I smiled. Despite my frustration at not cracking this case, Errol had a way of always cheering me up.

"Let's lay out the facts: four victims—a gaffer, a grip, a DP, and a cutter. Plus, the attempt on Ingrid. We know they all worked together on *Iron Horse*. But even though it's been lost, McSweeney doesn't give a fig. So he's clearly not our man."

"And Goldstein? Seems solid he offed Hugh. And I'd *love* to send him to the cooler. Wonder if those striped suits will freeze?"

"Hmm. Not a bad idea."

I set down my cup and seized Errol's.

"Uh . . . what?"

"Nail Goldstein. See if he'll gab about Mammoth. Even if he doesn't, we can still bring him in on first-degree murder."

"You're allowed to nab crooks?"

"Better believe it, Jack." I checked myself in the mirror which was one one-hundredth of Ingrid's. Then I checked my bag. Everything I needed was there. "Culver City?" I asked like a blue-nose.

"Yes, M'lady." Errol bowed. "Please allow me to escort you."

The fun and games stopped the minute we hit Goldstein's garage. His office was in a swanky building, close enough to the studios and Beverly Hills. I imagined him dining at Chasen's, ordering chili extra hot. We walked from the lot to the lobby. Another bulldog. And yes, she was blonde.

"Good morning," I said with a cheer I didn't feel. "We're here to see Mr. Goldstein." She looked up blankly from her semi-circular desk. "Attorney-at-Law," I clarified.

"Oh!" Had somebody goosed her? "Do you have an appointment?"

"Sure," I said. "Tell him Hughley sent me."

She got on the blower and turned away. I thought I heard angry blasts from the other end.

"Very well," she said primly. "You may go up. But him—" She pointed at Errol.

"He comes with me. The kid stays in the picture."

She waved a languorous hand: either to direct us to the elevator or implore us to be gone.

We stopped on Goldstein's floor. Errol might not know it but I certainly did.

When we opened the door to his office, we met not another gatekeeper but Howie himself. He looked red in the face, his eyes blazing as he led us inside and slammed his inner door.

"What's this hooey about Hughley?" he yelled, whirling toward us.

"Thanks, don't mind if I do."

I sat in one of those plush guest chairs, then nodded to Errol to do the same.

"It's not hooey. But before we get to that, let me introduce my partner, Errol. Errol uh Hughley."

"And I'm Eisenhower! Is this some kind of shakedown?"

Goldstein stood before his desk, mercifully bereft of carved lions. I shot a glance to his framed degrees. USC. Figured.

"No, Mr. Goldstein. And you should remember Errol."

He squinted.

"You're the egg?"

Errol nodded.

"I picked up lots of colorful language from you. Howie?"

"What do you two shysters want?"

"Isn't that your job?" I asked.

"Can the funny stuff. I can tell you that giant lizard doesn't get a penny even if he calls himself Rockefeller. As for you, Forenza, *I'll* decide the time of your payoff, and not before."

"This might seem amazing, Howie, but we're not here to talk about money." His eyes bulged in shock. "We're here about Hughley. And his tragic demise."

"Insurance already investigated!" he yelled. "What's there to know? He took a big risk like always and ended up hamburger meat!"

I winced.

"My partner and I were recently at Clover Airfield. We talked to a mechanic named Owen—know him?"

Goldstein sniffed.

"Certainly not!"

"Well, he knew you. Says you were there to watch Hughley's plane take off."

"So? Lots of people were. This was a newsworthy, experimental flight."

"According to Owen, when you heard about the crash, you didn't exactly cry the L.A. River. In fact, you seemed kind of happy."

"*Absolute bunk!*" Goldstein yelled, pausing to take off his jacket. I noted this with interest. Lawyers tended to wear three-piece suits even in the shower.

"Is it?" I asked cooly. "What do you make of this?" I shoved the copy I'd made from the insurance. Goldstein's beach-tanned face went white.

"Fine. You got me." He tried to appear calm, but I could see sweat on his dress shirt. He loosened his tie. "What's it gonna take? I'm due to get the five mil. Look, I'll split it with you, 50/50."

"I'm not looking for dough. Lenski gave me plenty. I'm looking for justice. But I'll put in a good word for you if you chirp to me about Mammoth."

I studied his face. He looked genuinely puzzled.

"I don't know what you mean. I'm not on retainer, and I haven't handled their business in years." He wiped his brow. "More's the pity."

"The names Felize, Alexander, Haskell, and McGee mean nothing to you?" He shook his head. "But you've heard of Ingrid Johansson?"

Howie whistled.

"Who hasn't? What a doll! But what does she want with me?"

I glanced over at Errol. We'd come to the same conclusion. Goldstein might have conspired to blip Hughley, but as far as Mammoth was concerned, he was smelling like Ivory Soap. In other words: he wasn't the studio killer.

"Errol?"

He rose heavily, pinning Howie's hands behind his back.

The attorney objected.

"Now, wait just a second! I want to speak to my lawyer!"

I shook my head. Only in this town could you have a lawyer's lawyer.

"They're be time for that at the station," I said, snapping open my bag to snap a pair of handcuffs on him.

"You can't arrest me!" he yelled. "You aren't a cop!"

"Contrary to popular belief, Mr. Goldstein, I can. And for your information, I used to be one."

That shut him up.

With Errol still "escorting" him, we hustled him downstairs and into the Ford.

"You call this an automobile?" he sneered from the passenger seat.

"It's not a Rolls," I said, "But it gets you to where you're going." I turned to face him. "And you're going downtown."

Howie stopped his whining somewhere around Mid-City, but the hour's drive still felt like a year. I left the Ford idling at the curb by City Hall, leaving Howie and Errol together. I'm sure that went well.

When I stepped to the LAPD front desk (the place where I'd met Bill!), I confess I was let down he wasn't there. But after the john on duty made a couple of calls on his handheld radio, it wasn't long before Bill strode in, looking more handsome than ever in his crisp uniform. When I saw him, I blushed. After all, we'd just—

"Nicky!" he called with a smile, then gave me a wink. "Any stars I should nab?"

"No, but I do have a lawyer. He confessed to killing Hughley."

"*The* Hughley?" he gasped. "As in planes and pictures?"

"The same. Sadly for him, his shyster is a louse. Had him blipped for five mil." Bill's eyes widened. "Insurance." I handed over the paper.

"Jeepers, Nicky, you should come back to the force!. We'd sure pinch a lot of bad guys."

I forced a grin.

"You know where they put dames. And it's not in a black-and-white."

He sighed.

"A shame. They'd be naming this place after you."

"Oh, I almost forgot. The creep's in my car out front." He gave me a look. "With Errol."

Bill let out a laugh.

"Then, everything's jake."

"Yeah. And Bill, would you mind not telling the *Times*? I never thought I'd sound like Manly, but I don't want the publicity. Not with four freshly dug graves. I need to go about my business without being tailed by newshawks."

He nodded.

"Sure, Nicky. Uh... when can I see you again? Another club date?"

I smiled.

"We'll see. Who knows when I'll be in need of a dreamboat?"

It was hard to say who blushed harder on the way out the station. But I'd venture that Bill won.

Chapter 33
Wescott and Spencer

A fter we'd made our "quiet" arrest, I felt beat and drove to my joint. Even Errol looked all in, throwing himself across the couch with a groan.

"Coffee?" I asked, throwing down my bag. Again, it had come handy.

"You betcha. Just a splash of cream."

"Milksop."

"Tough broad."

We both grinned. I realized I got along better with Errol than just about anyone. Excluding Bill.

I plopped down on a rickety chair.

"So," I sighed, "now that Goldstein's cleared from all the rub-outs at Mammoth, what does that leave us?"

I frowned.

"What about Wescott?" asked Errol.

"What about her? She's making McSweeney. No secrets there."

"I know," he said, getting up for another cup. "I mean, she's with him now and she was with Hughley. She's one of the few picture people at Mammoth who knew that screwy bird."

I shrugged.

"You said that broad's so cold she makes Connecticut look like Mexico. She's just not the type of dame to get mixed up in murder. Hell, she's practically royalty."

"Yeah," he conceded, "born and bred a Yankee with a doctor for a father. Attended Bryn Mawr. Plays tennis and golf like a pro. Disturbingly athletic."

"Hmm. Isn't she supposed to be smart?"

"That's like asking if Hoover is dumb. *Of course!* Did you know she sold Lenski the rights to *Pittsburgh Story?* Then finagled it so she'd star. Two Oscars, despite being "box office poison," and there you go. She does it all so well—why not murder?"

"I might buy she was in with Goldstein, but union crew? Why'd she want to ice guys a million times below her pay grade?"

"Oh. I should mention. They say she's with Tracy Spenser now."

"WHAT?"

How many men did this tootsie leave in her wake? Probably more than the Shamrock!

"She's done with McSweeney. Doesn't want to hurt the wife. But guess what?"

I put a hand to my head.

"Hit me."

"Spenser's married too. And his wife—get this—is another devout Catholic!"

In the Vatican somewhere, the Pope was shedding tears.

"So, she's a bit of a floozy. Name me one actress who isn't."

Errol looked up to the ceiling.

"Donna Reed," he intoned, clasping his claws.

"Maybe *she* did it," I growled, tired of Hollywood gossip.

"Oh no," said Errol solemnly, "she's just about perfect." He frowned. "Not like Young Loretta."

"Please . . . don't tell me," I begged. "I'll have to take another shower."

"Let's get back to Wescott."

"Like I said, I don't see it."

Errol sat up.

"She's known as this cold dame who slums around in trousers. But behind the scenes, she's hotter than Lana Turner!"

"And?"

"She likes powerful men: Hughley, McSweeney. She left one for the other. Maybe she helped off Hughley and got McSweeney's "revenge" for *Iron Horse.*"

"That doesn't make sense!" I cried. "McSweeney says he was fine."

"But what does he say," Errol asked, "under the covers?"

"How should I know?!" I cried. "All I heard were moans!" We put our cups down the sagging wood that passed for a living room table. "What now?" I asked. "I don't think I can take another sea voyage."

Errol waved a claw.

"Not necessary. I read in *Movie Show* Wescott's filming right now. And guess who's her co-star?"

"Freida Braun?"

He laughed.

"No! Tracy Spencer. She likes to keep 'em close."

"What studio?"

"Guess."

I sighed.

"So it's back to Mammoth? At least we can get through the gate."

My old friend wasn't there, but when they called up Lenski's office, I was given a literal pass. I guess I'd have to stop in later to update him on the case. That's why I hoped against hope we'd find something on Wescott.

The set we entered was somewhat of a letdown. Compared to the glory of Western and New York Streets, it seemed kind of drab: just the interior of some apartment. Of course, it was the kind I could never afford with its art deco polished black floor and furniture direct from Bullock's on Wilshire. Still, as I lurked in the shadows with Errol, I really hoped we could get Wescott aside and question her.

The director, a calm, balding man with glasses, finished futzing with the lights and called his players on set. Wescott was dressed in a sharp sweater and those famous linen trousers, while her co-star (presumably Spenser) slumped at a kitchen table in a dark natty suit.

"SPEED!" The director called.

"SPEED," came from the soundman wearing headphones.

"AND, ACTION!"

Just like in the movies, a clapboard clacked, and Wescott and Spenser were off on what they were known for: crackling, witty dialogue and a not-so-subtle battle of the sexes. It seemed the plot had something to do with Wescott going up against Spenser in court. They bantered for what seemed like ages until the goofy male neighbor appeared to sit down at the piano and yodel a love song to Wescott.

My attention started to drift until Errol elbowed my ribs. This whole process of shooting, with its multiple takes and resetting of lights, could drive anyone to drink. And that's what Spenser did, removing a flask from his breast pocket to take a few hearty sips.

"Is it always this boring?" I whispered to Errol.

He looked like I'd insulted his mother.

"Boring?" he asked incredulously. "This is magic happening here! Thousands will be transfixed in theatres across the nation!"

"Okay, pipe down. You sound like Mammoth Publicity."

"If only," he breathed, near-literal stars in his eyes.

"Let's corner Wescott," I said. "Before she jumps on Spenser."

"We better leg it quick then."

I used mine to approach the actress who was getting a power puff in the face.

Oh, the glamor!

"Miss Wescott," I nodded. Her attention was on her paramour who continued to imbibe.

"Yaahs?" she said, in that nails-on-chalkboard Connecticut drawl.

I produced my license.

"I'm working for Mr. Lenski. Have a few minutes?"

"For Mr. Lenski, sure," she said, leaning forward, her angular features curiously attractive. "He's been good to me."

"Well." I lowered my voice. "You may have heard there's been a series of murders on the lot."

"Oh my! I knew about Ingrid, but . . . murders?"

Even Spenser looked up.

"Yes. Let me ask you this: Did you know a Larry Felize?"

"Of course!" She clapped her hands together. Even offscreen, she seemed to be acting. "A lovely man! He used to tell stories about his unit in the Great War. He even met Patton!"

"Oh."

I had assumed this highbrow dame would lower her nose at the crew, but here she was, just one of the guys!

"How about Tony Alexander?"

"Oh yes. He was a grip, correct? He used to make the most brilliant tea."

I moved past the faux-British affectation.

"What about Patrick Magee and Wes Haskel?"

She put a thin, large hand under her pointed chin.

"I don't know the first, but Haskel? Never worked with him but he's said to be a genius. 'A painterly sensibility.' You don't mean to say he's dead?"

"They all are," I answered. I moved in for the slash to the jugular. "Along with Hughley."

Wescott seemed to lose a bit of her cool—maybe 10 degrees—but then recovered.

"Poor Hugh," she sighed, "I told him not to go up in that aeroplane."

"Why?" asked Errol. Wescott looked at him for the first time.

"Fame and Flame?" she asked.

"Right."

"I understand it's about to start production."

"Yes," I said, "and Errol here follows the Method."

"How curious," Wescott drawled, withdrawing her gaze from Errol before remembering his question.

"That aeroplane was a prototype—some kind of experiment. If it had worked, it could have helped our dear boys." She sighed. "But it didn't, and now poor Hugh is gone. I told him not to take such personal risks."

"Let some other pilot die?" I asked.

"Well . . . yes. He was the owner of the company. It was his job to hire employees who would assume the risks for him."

"Like your stunt double?" I asked.

Wescott frosted over like a windshield in winter.

"I have none," she said primly. "I do all of mine myself."

"Peachy. Miss Wescott: Is there any connection between those four dead souls and Mr. Hughley? Besides yourself, of course."

She looked offended, but then, she usually did.

"I have no idea, Miss—?"

"Forenza."

"Hughley owned his own studio, you know," she said in her superior tone.

"Yes, he bought RKO. So, it's quite possible he knew one or more of the victims."

"I suppose so. Look, Miss Forenza—what exactly are you driving at?"

"What if I told you Hughley's death was no accident? That it was rigged by his lawyer to cash in on insurance."

"How horrid!" Wescott cried. Tears began to form in the corners of her eyes. Was she acting, or was this real?

"Are you acquainted with Howard Goldstein?"

"Hugh mentioned him one time or other—said he didn't trust him."

"He shouldn't have."

"Don't you think you should inform the police?"

"I've done better than that," I said, thinking of Bill.

"Well . . . what's their theory?"

"That the murders may or not be connected. They're on the prowl right now."

I looked at her face—nothing.

Acting again?

Wescott shook her head, light curls falling over her shoulder.

"I sincerely hope they find the culprit," she said. "I've dealt with murder on film, of course, but never in reality. Isn't that right, Tracy?"

Her companion looked up and smirked. He was now three sheets to the wind.

"One more thing. Mickey McSweeney."

"What about him?"

Now Wescott's tone became hard—harder.

"It may be a coincidence, but all the studio victims worked *The Iron Horse*. Has he ever mentioned this picture to you—say, in a private setting?"

Wescott's porcelain skin paled.

"I don't know what you're implying," she said primly. "I'm barely acquainted with Mr. McSweeney."

I put out a metaphoric foot, waiting for it to be stepped on.

"That's not what I heard."

"Oh!" She waved a theatrical hand, playing to the last row. "The Hollywood rumor mill! If you believed that, I'd be pregnant and married several times over!"

"I meant, I *heard* it. On the *Shamrock*. Your little tryst below deck."

Wescott rose hastily. Now, she was playing to the camera.

"I don't know what you're getting at. Yes, I was involved with Mickey. I seem to be attracted to Irishmen who can't put down the booze."

I looked at Spenser, now asleep, his head on the prop table.

"Habits can be changed," I said. "What I want to know is this: Did McSweeney ever express anger at *Iron Horse* being lost?"

Wescott thought.

"No. Never. Wait." I did. "There was a time in Mexico—it was quite a fiesta. And then, out of the blue, he said, 'You know, after I die, they won't know my greatest picture. That bastard Lenski melted it down for silver."

I exchanged a glance with Errol.

"And, to your knowledge, did he ever act on this feeling?"

"What do you mean?"

"Revenge," I said calmly.

"Are you implying he's a murderer?!"

She was going for that third Oscar.

"I'm a PI, Miss Wescott. It's my job to consider everything, no matter how unpleasant."

She calmed down, preparing to play the big crying scene.

"You don't know Mickey," she said, wiping away the tears now cascading down to her chin. "He comes on tough, but he wouldn't hurt a fly. He's fought for this country—"

Filmed it, I corrected silently.

"—and he loves his crews. He should-should sue you for defamation!"

"Save the drama for the screen, Miss Wescott. One last question. Did you take it upon yourself to seek his revenge for *him?*"

"Well! I-I never—Spenser, did you hear what this coarse woman said? Spenser, wake up!"

"Thanks for your time, Miss Wescott. You've been more than kind."

Errol jumped in.

"Hope this picture does boffo BO!" he cried.

Chapter 34
Anatomy of a Shooting

"Time to see Lenski," I said, traipsing with Errol out of the bright set and into the brighter air. November—and not a cloud in the sky. "Never keep the client in the dark."

"That's what Ellery Queen says," he nodded.

We were by the Overland entrance: a good way from Thalberg by foot. Then one of those golf carts whizzed by.

"Think we can catch a ride?" I asked Errol.

"Oh no!" he said, shocked. "If you take more than one passenger, you have to call Transportation."

"I'm for unions," I said. "They prevent exploitation. But sometimes the rules seem to go just a tad too far."

With a sigh, I motioned to Errol, and we traipsed across Lot 1. By now, the novelty of standing sets, lakes, and tanks had lost their appeal. But not for Errol. I practically had to drag him past medieval France and a Spanish hacienda.

"Can we get there today?" I mumbled, but I really wasn't sore. *Let the guy have his dream.* God knows most of mine had died.

Panting, I led him toward Thalberg with its stately white columns like a set of the Supreme Court. In the distance, I spotted the Mammoth water tower. This place was like its own city: I'd spotted a post office, a hospital, and had seen the fire department in action.

You never have to leave, I thought. *Bunk down on a prop bed, and call the studio home.*

It was easier this time to get past the bulldog in the lobby. She even escorted us to open the upper floor's door. As she retreated, I stared at Lenski's assistant. This dame was different from the one I'd seen just a week ago.

"Is Mr. Lenski available?" I asked.

"And who may I say is here?"

Whom, I thought. That pesky UCLA.

"Nicky Forenza and Errol, uh, Forenza."

"How sweet," he muttered, "for you to adopt me!"

"Just a moment." This new gal buzzed Lenski and gave him the news. When she hung up, she pointed to his tall door. "Go in," she ordered.

This one needed some polish: a thick coat of 'pleases' and 'thank-yous.'"

Once again, I made the long walk to Lenski's desk, considering how such a small man had gained such enormous power. It wasn't through Ma's Chicken Soup.

"Well?" he said, folding his hands over a contract. Errol had told me they were up in seven years. Another poor sap tied to the wheel.

I updated him on everything we'd found so far, omitting Hughley's murder. Even Lenski might bring the cops in on that one.

"The Iron Horse?" Lenski wrinkled his forehead. "I remember most pictchas, but not that one. All I can tell you is McSweeney is a fine director. Wish he would work for me more."

"Mr. Lenski, what about Catherine Westcott? When she was uh with McSweeney, think she fell so hard she did his dirty work for him?"

"I trust no one," Lenski said. "That's why I'm here and not Thalberg."

"He died of heart disease," said Errol.

"So they say."

I soared right over this one.

"What about Wescott?"

The mogul chuckled, lighting up a Cuban cigar. A pungent waft of white smoke covered the top of his head.

"You're good at this game, Forenza. Born to be a PI." *Not really*, I thought, but didn't speak. Lenski leaned back, cigar still in his mouth. "Nah," he finally said. "That high-class dame ain't got it in here." He pointed to his chrome dome. "She's one of those liberal types who voted for Upton Sinclair."

I nodded. I'd been at school then, but knew him as a socialist. The dirtiest word in J. Edgar's—and clearly Lenski's—vocabulary.

"Even Democrats can kill," I said.

Lenski waved a dismissive hand.

"You don't know this dame. She wouldn't lower herself to wipe food from her own face. She's one of those back East bluenoses. The best schools and all that." He grinned. "Personally, I think she stinks as an actress—too mannered—but after a tough start, the public seems to love her."

"I see. So, in your view, she's not a killer? She must be clever, though."

"Her kind of smarts is taught at those swanky girl schools—where they teach good posture. Besides, this girl has seen more beds than a maid at the Ambassador. McSweeney was nothing special."

I looked down.

Another suspect—cleared.

"Mr. Lenski," I said, "I wouldn't be doing right by you if I didn't question the bird who shot Alexander."

"No publicity!" Lenski yelled, his cry as natural as breathing.

"There will be none," I said. "Promise. But I need to know what he knows."

I hoped Lenski wouldn't stage another "heart attack." Instead, he nodded.

"All right," he said, waving around his cigar. "He's on suspension now—you can guess why. My girl can give you his home address."

"Thanks. Uh, Mr. Lenski—what happened to the old one?"

"Oh! She's VP of Story now."

"That was fast," I said.

"So was she."

I made the long walk out, pausing to get the address.

This must be, I thought, *the only business on earth where you could go from secretary to VP inside a week.*

Nice work if you could get it.

Chapter 35
Eating at the Hat

We hoofed it to the Ford, which thankfully started up. I was on a mission to head for the Hollywood Hills when Errol stopped me.

"Uh, Nicky," he said, stooping in the passenger seat. "Can I ask a favor?"

"You need dough?" I asked. "No problem with Lenski's stash."

"Well. No." He sounded embarrassed, like his suit no longer fit. "It's just . . . ever since I hatched, I've wanted to go to the Hat."

I turned to him as I turned right onto Washington.

"You don't like yours?"

"No, I like it fine. I mean . . . the Hat. You know, the one you eat at?"

I chuckled.

"The Brown Derby?"

"Yeah! That's it. Nicky . . . please. Then we can grill that director."

I smiled. It'd been a while since Alexander left us. If we waited an hour or two, it shouldn't make a big difference.

"All right."

I decided to take La Brea, then a right on Wilshire, and a left on Rossmore which turned into Vine. You couldn't miss our destination. There it sat, a rounded brown lump, in the unmistakable shape of a hat. Just to drive the point home, there was also a sign shaped like a hat on the restaurant's crown.

"I can't wait!" Errol bounced up and down, head hitting the roof.

"Careful there," I said, "don't make this jalopy into a Burbank top."

I didn't know if he heard me since he exited the Ford as soon as I came to a stop. I sighed. This luncheon would put me back some. Good thing I had Lenski's envelope.

When we swung through the door, I did in fact feel I was inside a giant hat. The host, seeing Errol in his "costume," nearly fell over himself to seat us. We were surrounded by caricatures of all the stars who must frequent this place: I recognized Johansson, Wescott, and Spencer.

"We've got to try the Cobb Salad!" Errol enthused, putting aside his menu. "And the famous pumpernickel!"

"If you say so," I smiled. For once, I could relax, not searching for clues or looking around suspicious. For a short time, I could just be Nicky; not Nicky Forenza, PI, and I let out a deep, calm breath. When I'd first taken up Guiseppe's offer, I didn't realize this racket was 24-7. Would I agree to take over for him now? Probably, I thought. A woman in the LAPD was like a putting lipstick on Errol. Utterly useless, the task disappointing.

We placed our orders with a waitress so ingratiating I wanted to tip her now. In a jif, out came our coffees, salads, and bread, and I grudgingly had to agree this food was excellent: though pricey beyond my usual means.

"What do you think?" Errol cried, a piece of lettuce hanging from his mouth.

"For bunny food, it's tasty. And the bread is the best I've had."

"See?" Errol pointed his fork. "Toldya!"

"Any stars here I should be aware of?" I asked. Not that I cared, but I knew *he* did.

"Oh yes! There's the two leading gossip columnists!"

I looked over. All I could see were two enormous hats. Fitting.

"And there's Francis LaRue—she only allows them to film her from her good side—and that's Mary O'Hara—jeepers, her hair is as red in person as it is in Technicolor! And—"

"Okay, I get the picture."

In fact, I was sick of pictures, or "pictchas," as studio folk called them. If I never saw another film in my life . . .

"We've *got* to have the Grapefruit Cake!" Errol nearly shouted.

"Sounds ghastly."

"Oh no! It was made for Freida Braun and they say it's delicious!" As our waitress hovered over him, he pointed to the menu. "Two please!"

"You don't want to share?" I ask.

"Not on your life!"

When the two small plates came, their contents really were a delight: a delicate chiffon cake topped with cream cheese and a light grapefruit graze. I ate mine to the last crumb, which was odd, since I hated grapefruit!

"Happy now?" I asked Errol as I paid the check. The tab was more than I made at Lockheed—in a week!

"Thanks, Nicky," he said, as we swung out and into the Ford. "That's another landmark I can cross off my list."

I hoped the next wasn't Crossroads of the World, where they sold souvenirs so tacky even tourists wouldn't buy them. Before we drove away, I took one last look at the Derby. In what other town, I wondered, could you find an eatery shaped like a giant hat?

I sighed.

Only in L.A.

Chapter 36
The Hollywood Hills

"I don't think she's gonna make it," I hissed to Errol, making a similar sound to the old Ford's sputtering engine.

Why build homes, I wondered, *on hills so steep you had to be dropped there by aircraft?*

The answer was simple: to lord it over the little people living down on the flats. The Ford nearly rolled over and put up its wheels before I turned it off.

"Better turn your wheels into the curb," Errol said. "Or you could end up getting a free song from Judy."

"To hell with it. Let the old girl rest for a while."

"They why are you getting out?"

"Cute," I growled. "Very cute."

We had climbed our way past mansions that put Sunset to shame: French chateaus, English Tudors, Spanish haciendas, and merely *huge:* like 25,000 square feet big.

What did they do with so much space? I wondered. *There were only so many orgies you could hold at one time.*

As Errol and I fought our way to the door (this hill was like the Sierras), I have to say I was a bit disappointed. Sure, it had more columns than Tara but was probably only a modest 10,000 square feet.

We knocked. A uniformed butler answered.

Why was I surprised? I realized then, to my embarrassment, I didn't know the director's name!

"Uh," I began, "we're here for Mr. Lenski." I flashed my license. "Just want to ask the owner a few questions."

"Very well," huffed the butler, who naturally was English. "Wait here." He offered no seats, just left us hanging in a foyer more suited to Versailles.

"What's this bird's name?" I whispered to Errol.

"William Weller," he whispered back. "He's had an affair with Ruth Davis, but guess he doesn't cut his wife as much slack."

"Maybe."

A jaunty man bounced in wearing tennis whites and holding a racket. Though he was in his fifties, his body looked like a twenty-year-old's. Must have played tennis *a lot*.

"Afternoon!" he barked gruffly, though I don't think he was steamed. "Come in, come in!" He gave Errol the once-over. *"Fire and Flame?"* he asked.

"Uh, 'Fame.'"

"Of course." He ushered us into what polite society called "a drawing room." "Please, sit down. Like a drink? Timothy can fix you one."

As Errol opened his mouth to assent, I shook my head.

"Thanks but no thanks, Mr. Weller. I try not to drink on the job."

"Well, I'll have one." He snapped his fingers to summon the butler, then sat across from us on what I guessed you'd call a "divan." A tumbler was in his hand faster than Superman could fly. "Timothy tells me you're a PI sent by the boss. Frankly, I don't see why. He knows the whole story."

"Which is—?" I prompted.

"I knew Mildred was stepping out on me with the small stuff: mainly crew. There must have been at least a dozen."

I'd like to meet this Mildred—find out her secret. "Anyway, this Alexander was different. She seemed really taken with him, though he was just a grip." He snorted. "I make a hundred times as much."

Ah, the second piston of the twin Hollywood Engine. Money. The first one was Fame.

"I'm sure this is tough to talk about—" I said.

He laughed and waved a hand.

"Oh no, not at all. I've had my share of tête-à-têtes."

That's one way to put it, I thought.

"What do you think," I asked, "attracted her to Alexander?"

"His looks, I suppose. I may be rich but I'm no Brock Powell."

"Few are. That's why he's the King."

Weller laughed.

"You've got a point. Anyway, the rumor mill started to fly about Mildred and Tony, and how I was consumed with jealous rage."

"Were you?" asked Errol.

"At first. But when I started dating that dish—"

"—who is?" I interrupted.

"A gentleman never talks. Let's just say she knows her way around a bed."

"A pro?" I asked, relishing my double entendre.

"Nope. Married to one. Of a kind. Some gaffer."

Errol's eyes met mine.

Could this mattress jockey possibly be Mrs. Felize?

"What happened at the commissary?" I asked, trying to get my snooping on track. "Were you there for the shooting?"

Now Weller guffawed.

"Nah! I was in the East Indies, shooting a picture. And a damned fine one it is!"

"I'm sure." Now came the sucker punch. "Do you know who killed Alexander?"

"How could I? I was out of the country."

"And Mildred?"

"She was heartbroken. Drove to a spa in Palm Springs."

"I'm sure she's grieving there," I said, thinking of Swedish massage and mud facials.

"Does *she* know who killed her lover?"

"She wouldn't say. She was just so broken up."

"Well, thanks for your time, Mr. Weller." I stood, wishing now for that drink. "Errol?" I nodded for him to trail me past the stained-glass door.

Wellers' joint, I contemplated, *wasn't exactly a place of worship.*

"Well?" Errol asked.

We inched our way down the driveway. I wished for some rope and crampons.

"Well, I sighed."

Unfortunately, the Ford was still there. Hadn't rolled into some pool.

"How'd you like," I asked, sliding into the driver's seat, "to take a trip to Palm Springs?"

Chapter 37
Among the Whispering Palms

"Thanks so much for coming," I told Bill, slipping into the seat of his black-and-white. "No fancy machines today?"

"Afraid not," he said from the driver's seat. "But if the Chief finds out I'm taking this jalopy out of town, he just might have kittens."

"I'll never tell," I smiled, looking in the rearview mirror to see an indignant Errol. He stared at us from behind what looked like a cage.

"I feel like a punk," he protested, "on his way to the cooler."

"If you don't pipe down, you might be."

He huffed, turning to a stack of movie magazines. He was slid down far in his seat so his head didn't hit the roof.

"So," said Bill. "Haven't heard from you since the Grove."

"I know," I groaned, "this case has me going in circles."

"Anything you can share?"

"Well . . . all my suspects seem to have an air-tight alibi—*if* they're telling the truth."

"And are they?"

"Who knows? Mrs. Felize's been with half of Hollywood—talk about one degree of separation!"

He chuckled.

"She seems to weave in and out of this thing. Then there's the equally active actress who's forgotten who she is. She might be playing a role, or she might be for real. Lenski vouches for her. Then . . ." I took a deep breath, "there's two directors, both of them big. They get around too, but one has a connection to all four victims and the other has a good reason—to turn a grip into a stiff."

"Wow!"

"The only one who's guilty is Hughley's shyster. But did he have help? And did he or a studio hack blip the four others?"

Bill exhaled.

"It's a good thing you're the peeper and not me. I'm just a regular beat cop and I think I'll stay that way."

"You don't want to solve crime? Have your neck twisted a hundred different ways while you try to figure things out?"

"No, thanks."

"Could you keep it down up there?" Errol asked. "Some of us are trying to read."

Bill nodded toward the back.

"He's not really an actor, is he? Those scales are just too real."

I hesitated, but since he was helping us, I thought he deserved the truth.

"No. He's an actual dragon. Hughley found him—at uh, the earth's core."

"Always heard he was kind of screwy."

"Errol, or Hughley?"

"*Hey!*" Errol shouted.

Bill and I exchanged a grin. I took comfort in the fact he knew how to get out of L.A. *I* had never gone further than Woodland Hills in the Valley.

"What is this?" I asked as we headed north past some place called Santa Clarita Valley. Talk about desolate! Then Bill took something called the Pearblossom Highway past small towns surrounded by nothing but sand. He called it "the high desert." To me, it was just sand. We went through Victorville, Apple Valley *(who in their right mind would live here?)*, Johnson Valley, and finally, Coachella Valley. I was one Valley away from insanity, until I saw a sign for something called "Twenty-Nine Palms."

"They couldn't make it an even thirty?" I asked.

Finally, we pulled into Palm Springs. Here, there was more sand, sprinkled with some very nice resorts.

"We did it!" Errol shouted, doing his best to bounce. "We beat the two-hour rule!"

"The what?" I asked.

"Stars are allowed to come here since they can get back to the studio in two-hours—for reshoots. Really, Nicky, don't you *read?*"

"Not *your* yellow rags," I said, wiping sweat from my forehead. If L.A. was hot, this place was twenty degrees hotter. "Water," I croaked, as Bill stopped before a hotel that looked like an old Spanish Mission.

I wasn't far off: the sign read "Spanish Inn." Once Errol saw it, he slid out the black-and-white as if he were on skates.

"Don't tell me," I said. "Something to do with Hollywood."

"All the big stars stay here," he gasped, "except the ones who have houses. Lana Turner, Esther Williams—"

"I get the picture."

Bill led me inside, blissfully cool after the arid drive. *And this was winter!* He politely asked for a room, describing Errol as "our young child." *Thank God we'd left him outside!* If he'd heard that one, he would have flamed us into ash.

"You're in luck," the desk girl smiled, taking in too much of Bill in his crisply pressed uniform. "Most of our regular stars are back in L.A. shooting."

Poor Errol!

We went back to the front, where Bill moved his jalopy closer to our room.

"Come along, Junior," I told Errol.

He looked puzzled as we pulled a trunk from the trunk, then walked into our room. I, to my shame, didn't possess a suitcase, so I'd doubled up with Bill.

I looked around. This room was tops. I'd never stayed in a place like this: in fact, I'd never stayed anywhere. The extent of my world travels had been to the Valley and back, a distance of forty miles. Pops had never been flush and Ma stayed home with the kids. Fancy trips to joints like this were experienced only in theatres.

"Wow," Errol breathed, not having to duck for once since the ceiling was high. We were surrounded by white adobe, a ceiling fan cranking above. "It's just like *Casablanca!* Good thing Bogie's not here, though. He likes to tie one on. So . . . when do we hit the pool?"

He looked so eager he might have been my real child.

"Errol," I said, "we're here on business, remember?"

"Yeah, yeah. But you can't come to the Springs without taking a dip!"

I sighed, looking at Bill. He shrugged, then opened the clunky trunk to remove his swim trunks. He closed the door of the powder room, leaving me to change too. I glanced into the mirror—not bad. My polka-dot one-piece fit tightly without revealing too much.

"Va-va-voom!" whistled Errol. "More curves than Sunset!"

"Thanks," I blushed, rummaging for my coverup and buttoning up. Bill wasn't as modest: He emerged half-naked, better than any Tarzan. I couldn't speak—drool nearly ran down my chin!

"Careful, Lady Detective," said Errol. "Close that mouth before you catch sand fleas."

Bill laughed as Errol began to strip off.

"Uh," I said to the dragon, "how do we explain you? I don't think the Method applies to chlorine."

"Leave it to me," he winked, grabbing a large hotel towel.

I shot Bill a concerned look, but he spread his hands and led us back out. Shielding Errol with our bodies, we made it out back to the pool.

"Drag me in," he whispered, then lay down and went stiff.

He wasn't exactly light. Bill took his legs while I pushed his head. "Careful," he said, "you might need my brains someday." We positioned him by the steps as Bill floated him in. Removing my coverup, I waded in beside them.

"What are you supposed to be?" I hissed to Errol ."Some kind of pool toy?"

"Exactly," he grinned, freezing his face into that expression.

We floated him into the deep end, and I made a discovery: even covered with scales, a dragon made a swell raft! Bill and I clung to his side as we all enjoyed some much needed R&R."

"You look incredibly sexy," Bill whispered. "Better than Betty Grable!"

"That's what *he* said." I pointed to our impromptu floatie. "Maybe I'll insure my legs for a cool mil."

"You don't have to," Bill whispered, running a hand down my back. "To me, you're worth that and more."

"Can the sentiment," Errol growled, talking through a closed mouth. "What is this—a three-hankie weepie?"

"It will be if you don't stay still," I hissed.

"Isn't this swell?" Bill asked, giving a more-than-appreciative glance to what he could see of my cleavage. "I wonder what the poor people are doing?"

"What we always do," I said. "Work."

"Can you imagine," he asked, "living this life every day?"

Frankly, I couldn't. Pops owned a bodega—he was as far from the stars as we were here on Earth. And Ma spent her time in the kitchen—when she wasn't yelling at us kids. I'd never had aspirations of being Hollywood rich: especially now I'd been exposed to it. It seemed a vacuous lifestyle, full of hedonism but frankly not too much meaning.

"I hate to poop this party," I sighed, "but we need to get out and get down to business."

"Nicky's so dull," intoned Errol. "All work and no play."

"When this case is cracked," I said, "I'll take you to Santa Monica Pier." He frowned. "You can ride the carousel."

That seemed to improve his mood as we floated him back to the shallow end, over steps and then concrete. Once we'd rounded a white adobe corner, he took to his feet, shaking water from his scales directly onto me.

"Th-thanks," I sputtered.

"Welcome. Just remember: water is nicer than fire."

"So is a towel."

Bickering, we made our way back to the room where *I* took charge of the powder room. Once I was dressed and out, I saw Errol back in his suit and Bill in a polo shirt and rather tight shorts. Hubba hubba!

"Well, Errol," I asked, "what are the fancy-shmancy spas where Marge can heal her broken heart?"

"Well, the stars favor *The Oasis, The Palms, The Desert Sands, and the Hot Springs.*"

"What costs the most clams?"

"The Oasis, I think. They have—"

"You can button it. We'll see when we get there."

Errol sighed, but still got in the black-and-white along with Bill and me. Bill had a map (fancy that!) and it wasn't too long before we found the Oasis. Errol had been right. This was some swanky joint. There were more Rollses parked in the lot than there were in the Hollywood Hills.

We got out. Like most Hollywood hangouts, the exterior was bupkis: white, one-story, and boasting a barely visible sign. So the hoi polloi—like me—would be sure to pass it by.

"Errol—" I began.

"I know," he whined. "Junior stays in the car."

"Bill—"

"I'll keep him company—tell thrilling police stories."

"He'd like them better," I said, "if they were filmed for the screen."

I walked up to a white-awning entrance, and found, as always, some aspiring starlet.

"Do you have an appointment?" This one asked, hair perfectly coiffed and makeup flawless. Had some studio sent her?

"Uh, no," I said, trying to stay unflustered. "But I've heard . . . so much about this spa from my co-workers at Mammoth, I thought I'd stop by."

"Wonderful!" squealed this Ava-in-the-making, "you should try our Compleat Woman. It includes hydrotherapy, massage, weight loss magic, and a fruit facial!"

"Sounds . . . interesting," I said. "Tell you what—I'll just start with the water."

I'd be an Incompleat Woman if it saved me some jack.

"Right this way."

The white-coated woman rose, then led me into this sanctum of beauty. The first thing I did was scream: there was a woman before me in a white ghastly mask that made her look like the half man in the moon! This was attached to a hose which she held up proudly.

"Sorry," I half-mumbled, admonishing myself for nearly blowing my cover. I'd have to act like faces dressed in fruit salad was something I saw everyday.

"Here we are."

I stumbled past a young woman wearing a three-quarter mask festooned with . . . ice cubes? Once I saw they were plastic, I nearly relaxed, but what was the point of this torture? Pretending you were a Bacardi and Coke?

Thank all the Saints, the woman led me out back where several holes covered the ground.

"Mineral hot springs!" she chirped. "An ancient method of healing assured to make you feel youthful."

Sweetheart, I thought, *I only have ten years on you. And my boyfriend likes me just fine.*

I stared into the bubbling water.

"Do you have," I asked, "something I can wrap myself in?"

"Oh no," she giggled, "we're all women here. You're fine *au naturel.*"

You may be fine, I mused, *but I was raised Italian!*

That's why when I disrobed and plunged in, I still wore my bra and panties. Another woman, gorgeous, had no such compunctions, walking naked out of the spa and easing herself next to me.

"Hello," I said, wondering if that was something the rich would say.

"Afternoon." She bowed her blonde head toward me, curls so perfect it looked like she'd stepped from the set.

"Come here often?" I asked casually, averting my eyes from her Hollywood-perfect body.

"When I can. I've just returned from Monte Carlo."

"Oh. How were the tables?"

"Cool," she said, "I lost two-thousand on a single hand."

"Tough luck."

She waved a freshly manicured hand.

"It's all right. Phillip was there to spot me."

This was intriguing, but I had to start foxing around.

"Tell me," I said, "do you know a Marge Weller? She's an acquaintance of mine."

"Oh yes," said Blondie, examining her blood-red nails. "We've run into each other from time to time."

"How lovely. Does she favor this spa?"

Blondie frowned.

"Not that I know of." She smirked. "The Oasis is more her style."

What did that mean? Was it more or less flush?

"Well, I must be going," I drawled, rising to grab my clothes and a towel. "It was a pleasure."

"Indeed."

I'd have to remove my underthings to keep from getting soaked. Shoving them into my bag and hoping my .38 was waterproof, I stumbled my way back up front.

"Well, that was nice. I really do feel cured."

"Wonderful! What were you suffering from?"

"Tuberculosis," I said. "So, what do I owe you?"

"Oh! Nothing! It's on the house."

I thought that might be her reaction.

"Thanks."

I slumped my way back to my friends.

"Any luck?" asked Bill.

"No. But I met a blonde bombshell in the hot springs who gave me a clue."

I slid in next to Bill.

"How do you feel?" Errol asked from the back.

"Fine. Why do you ask?"

"Those springs are supposed to be healing."

I assessed my general health. In fact, I *did* feel more refreshed than when I'd first entered the spa. Would I admit this to Errol? The same time I'd tell him my dripping underthings were in my bag. In other words: *Never.*

"Where to?" asked Bill.

"The Oasis," I answered. He consulted the map, then drove past droves of sand to stop at the second spa. Now I was really starting to feel like a Hollywood star. "Wait for me," I mumbled, then approached another white-coated moppet. This time, I wasn't going to fool around.

"Mrs. Marge Weller," I said, flashing my license. "She here?"

The girl with Shirley Temple-like curls consulted her book.

"Oh. Yes. Right this way."

She escorted me past more fruit-salad-for-faces, *Phantom of the Opera* masks, and a contraption straight out of the Inquisition. We finally stopped before a mid-forties woman busily reading a magazine. Around her knees were two spring coils which looked like parts of an engine.

Was this spa, I wondered, *secretly working on weapons for the war?*

But I shook off this thought as I was introduced.

"Mrs. Weller," said the moppet, posing like Shirley at her worst, "this is uh, a private detective who wishes to speak to you."

I nodded until the moppet took the hint and left.

"Nicky Forenza," I said. "Mrs. Weller, may I ask the purpose of that machine?"

"Oh." She put down the magazine. "It's for weight loss. This is a massage chair."

"With rollers for hands?"

"I suppose you could say that. Now, Miss Forenza, what can I do for you?"

"I'm working for Lenski. And trying to put together how Tony Alexander died."

"Oh, poor Tony!" Marge made quite a show of her grief, even dabbing her eyes. "He was just a grip. Why would anyone shoot him?"

"That's what I'd like to know." I raised my voice to overcome the chair's groans. It sounded like an alley cat caught in a blender. "Mrs. Weller," I said, "it's no secret you and him were 'involved.' Did your husband, by chance, shoot Tony in a fit of jealousy? That's the Hollywood rumor."

"All rumors are true," she told me, "but not this one. William couldn't care less about my entanglements. If I'm not mistaken, he's got a new, young piece."

"Kim Felize."

"Whatever. We have a modern marriage: we both do what we want. As long as we're seen together at premieres and parties, it all works wonderfully."

"I'm sure."

I thought of Bill. If he ever stepped out on me with some sweet, young thing; the .38 in my bag would see the light of day. "You were close with Tony." I said. She nodded. "Is there anyone out there who'd want to see him knocked off?"

"He was a lovely man," Marge told me. "Polite, always smiling, and my, was he handsome! All the girls on the lot swooned when he came off the set." She smiled. "Before me, you can bet he had his share."

I nodded. Even Hollywood wives had the morals of a mare in heat.

"So, can you give me a name?"

"Well, there's Brock Powell."

"The actor?"

"Oh honey, he's more than that—the anointed 'King of Hollywood.'"

"But why . . . would such a huge star have it out for a grip?"

Marge shrugged, her legs jiggling under the coils.

"I told you. Tony was a dreamboat. And when Lilly Ford worked with him, well—let's just say there were sparks."

"So Powell had a thing for her?"

"The King doesn't like a peanut dipping his wick in his property."

I winced. These people were truly vile.

"So you think Powell bopped Tony?"

"Not personally, no! But you know that Tommy Manly? Chicago hood turned VP?"

I tried not to react.

"All too well."

"He's got the boys to do it. And make it look like it was my husband."

I nodded.

"Mrs. Weller, you've been very cooperative. Please get back to your ..."—"torture device" seemed harsh—"... coils. Thanks."

I tried not to run back to the black-and-white, and settled for a brisk walk.

"Bill! Errol!" I said, "we finally have something to go on!"

"A clue?" asked Errol.

"A big one. Bill—how fast can you get us back to L.A.?"

"Oh," he said, "in just about two hours."

Chapter 38
The Premiere

As we headed out past sand, I grilled Errol about Powell, learning about his musical start in the 1930s and how he got to be King.

"But Errol," I interjected, "what's he up to *now?*"

"He wrapped *Guns and Grief* in July. The premiere's tonight!"

I turned to watch him bounce.

"Where?" I asked.

"The greatest theatre of all!"

"You mean . . . the Paramount?"

"Oh, Nicky, no—Grauman's Chinese!" Now Errol couldn't stop blabbing about this hallowed ground. He told us it'd been around forever—or at least, since the Silents. Why Sid Grauman had chosen to build a pagoda in the middle of Hollywood Boulevard was a mystery even to him; still, it was *the* spot for premieres, and besides the Egyptian (also built by Sid), the *best* movie palace ever. "Think of the forecourt!" he cried.

"I'd rather not."

"All those footprints and handprints, from Mary Pickford to Judy to Powell! They've got—"

"We catch your drift," I said. "So, what time do we show up?"

"*7 P.M.!*" he shouted. "We should get there early. The crowds—"

"I know," I said dryly. "I read *Day of the Locusts.*"

"Never heard of it," he answered, "but you better get The Dress ready."

Bill chuckled.

"Looks like my good suit for me."

As promised, in less than two hours, Bill dropped us off at the Proctor. Despite living at their epicenter, I'd never gone to a premiere, and my nerves were on edge. *Nothing,* I thought, *a shot of Bacardi couldn't cure.*

Errol was so enthused I thought he might take flight. He absolutely insisted on helping me get dressed and even curled my hair! When I peered into my glass, bloodred lips staring back at me, I shrugged and concluded "Not bad."

"*Nicky, you're a bombshell!*" Errol cried, natty in his own suit. "Carrie Joanford should just retire."

Slipping into those painful gold heels, I made for the elevator, scaly publicist in tow. When the doors creaked open, we found Bill waiting downstairs.

"Nicky," he breathed, " you're an absolute knockout!" He bent to kiss my cheek.

"C'mon, Bill," Errol teased, "you can do better than that!"

"I'd smack her a big one, but don't want to smear that lipstick."

"Sure," I said, feeling the creep of a blush. Once Bill helped me get into my mink, we marched out the lobby, to—I thought—walk the short distance to the theatre. But Bill had other plans: he'd actually rented a limo! When a uniformed driver emerged to help us in and we were safely behind tinted glass, I could almost see the attraction of being treated like royalty.

We could see the premiere ahead before we'd even arrived. Huge klieg lights swept the sky, brighter than even the stars (the ones over our heads). That screwy pagoda was lit up in red neon, and by the time the limo crawled there, I saw hordes of people screaming like there'd just been an earthquake. They came from all walks of life: young girls clutching autograph books; dowdy matrons swooning when a favorite star walked by. They were seated on stands, the spillover jamming the sidewalks behind off-duty cops.

"Wish you were them?" I kidded Bill as the three of us stepped out. This caused a storm the likes of which was rarely seen in L.A.: flashbulbs sparked and fizzled as eager reporters moved in; vinyl books filled with signatures fluttered before our faces.

"*Who are they?*" I heard a shout.

"*Nobody!*" yelled a man, disappointment flattening the crowd like a giant hand. They immediately regained their pep: *A star was right behind us!* I heard her shouted name: *"Freida!"* but I doubt she'd recognize me, busy as she was absorbing waves of worship.

Publicity pushed us down the red carpet—to leave a wide space for Freida. I understood: she was bigger than life and needed to fill a whole frame. The crowd was now rushing forward, the cops forming a human barrier. Not wanting to be torn apart, I clung to Bill's hand tightly.

Finally, we arrived at the theatre doors, where a gossip gal in a hat interviewed the stars. *That's when I saw my chance.* Powell was next in line, on the arm of his new wife, and I was determined to nab him after The Hat was done.

Just my luck—The Hat nabbed Errol!

"See this amazing costume?" its owner cooed. "And how all the fans look forward to *Fire and Fame!*"

The pop of flashbulbs made Errol hide his eyes.

"Thanks," he choked out, while Bill and I subtly placed ourselves to make a Powell sandwich. I saw Publicity head our way like a Great White rolling its eyes. But now it was *my* time to strike!

"Mr. Powell," I said breathily to the imposing star. "Recognize this dress? Carrie Joanford wore it in *The Women.*"

He gave me an easy smile.

"Can't say I do," he drawled, "but I reckon you look just as good."

He gave me a wink. *What a wolf!* I saw his wife stamp her foot.

"Mr. Powell," I asked, "did you know Tony Alexander?" Now came the lie. "I'm asking for Mr. Manly."

At the dread name, the actor's dark eyes narrowed.

"Oh. Yes, he worked on the lot. He was on *Guns Ahoy!* with me and Carrie."

"Did you know he's dead?"

"Yes. Weller shot him in a fit of jealousy."

"Brock—" his wife whined. If I were her, I would have kept my hush since the lynx coat draped around her cost twice as much as Ma's house.

"They tell me," I went on smoothly, "it wasn't Weller at all. Mr. Powell, Meir Lenski wants answers. Was Alexander stepping out on Mrs. Weller's at the time of his death?"

Powell ran a hand through his dark, hanging fringe.

"I heard rumors," he said, "Tony was making Carrie."

"Did that upset you?" I asked.

He shrugged.

"At first. I thought he was beneath her salt. But she soon had—" he glanced at his wife, "—other means to keep her happy."

He gave me another wink. At least, I thought he did.

"Thanks so much, Mr. Powell. Good luck with the picture."

He ducked inside, engulfed by newshounds like Faust being pulled into Hell.

I sashayed off the red carpet, dragging Bill and Errol. My partner looked down in the mouth that we wouldn't stay for the flick. When we left, we walked down the boulevard, getting curious looks from those not overdressed, until we arrived at the Proctor, and then, my apartment.

"Well?" Bill asked as he removed my mink.

"I don't think Powell's guilty. He was trying to tell me—despite his wife—that he and Carrie are still on, and Tony was just a dalliance."

"Damn!" said Errol, flinging his hat on the couch. "I was hoping Powell was it."

"Why?" I asked, likewise throwing off my heels. "I thought you were a fan."

"I used to be," he sighed, "but now he's just in war pictures and the love stories are thin."

"*Errol!*" I cried with a smile at Bill. "Who knew you were such a romantic?"

"Uh..."

If dragons could blush, he did.

Chapter 39

Whodunit?

The next morning dawned hot and clear: Of course, it was L.A. I walked past Errol sprawled on the couch and covered his feet with a blanket. After all the excitement, I guessed he'd slept in, dreaming of Freida and concrete footprints.

I went over to my one window in an attempt to let in fresh air. The ancient fan in the corner just wasn't up to snuff. I stifled a yawn with one hand while cranking the glass with the other. I was hit with a breeze. The landlord was too chintzy to even give us screens. I leaned out, surveying the boulevard with its usual boozers and tourists. Just another day in Hollywood.

Except this time, it wasn't. As I turned back toward the kitchen, I heard a sharp sound. Must be some jalopy coughing. But then a sharp pain, as if Errol had flamed me, knifed into my side. Looking down, I saw my white housecoat stained with blood! Like always, I didn't go gracefully, falling onto a lamp which fell onto my table. Errol was up in a jiffy.

"What happ—?" he started, then saw the pooling blood. "Jumpin' Jehosaphat! We've got to get you to a doctor!"

I barely nodded, still in shock, I guessed.

"Queen," I gasped.

"Nicky, you are to me."

"Of Angels. On Vermont. Step on it."

He carried me into the elevator where I started to fade. When we hit the lobby, the telephone girl screamed, but it wasn't only at me: I saw Manly in a corner, scowling like one of his gangsters.

"Stop," he said. He was used to being obeyed.

"Are you certifiable?!" Errol cried. "We've got to get her to a hospital!"

"No." Manly was close-lipped today. He gestured with a hand that smelt faintly like cologne. "Take her back up." He punched the elevator button.

"But—"

"No buts," he said, unbuttoning his coat to reveal his waistband. From which he calmly displayed the curved wood grip of a gat. The door squeaked open as Manly handed the girl in the lobby what looked like a wad of dough. We all stumbled up to my door, which was open just a crack. "Where's the ameche?" Manly barked. "Need to call the studio doc." Errol nodded in its direction, prompting the goon to growl into it. "Put the broad down." He gestured to my bed. Errol, thoughtful as ever, laid down a towel so I wouldn't stain the mattress.

That's when I conked out. Don't know how long I was gone, but when I came to, I saw a kindly gray-haired man straight out of Central Casting.

"Well, hullo," he smiled. "I'm Doctor Martin from Mammoth."

I nodded weakly. If he'd told me he was going to operate now, on equipment supplied by the studio, I would have let him.

"How bad?" I croaked.

"Luckily, you were turned, so the bullet's point of entry was just above your hip."

"And that's good?"

"Oh, yes. It actually went *through* you." He rummaged in his black back to pull out a large gold pill. I started. Whoever he was, the shooter meant business. I craned my neck toward Manley, now lurking over me. "Who was it?" I asked.

"Don't know. Got my boys on it. Those you haven't iced or slipped into the icebox." He looked down with a glower. "This don't go no farther, capishe? I know you do, *Forenza.*"

"Why . . . hush?" I whispered, the pain turning me into a dope. "Not on . . . studio payroll."

Manly's face muscles didn't move.

"But you *were* working for us. For the boss. And if those newshounds catch on, they might sniff out *why.*" He showed his gleaming teeth. "Welcome to the Mammoth Family!" I closed my eyes, thinking I'd rather join his *other* Family. Manly addressed the room. "Listen up. Doc, you come by every day. Change the bandage or whatever. Forenza, so-called 'Errol'—neither of you take a power. Not until she's all healed up. Got me?" Everyone nodded—even me. But Manly couldn't leave until he made a threat. "If I hear tell you've flown," he told me, "I'll give you another pill. And dragon boy—" he turned to Errol. "Don't make me clip those wings."

Satisfied, he snapped at the doctor, and the two of them were gone.

"Did I really just hear," I asked Errol, "that we're not allowed to leave?"

He nodded.

"That heel is keeping us prisoner. Must've seen *Monte Cristo* a few too many times."

I touched my right side, now bandaged.

"Better listen," I said. "His family is *way* more connected than mine."

"Don't you worry, Nicky. I'll take care of you, same as you took care of me."

"No payoff," I half-grinned.

"None needed. This is strictly friendship. For my best friend in town and on earth." I reached out to pat his claw. I was no sob sister, but somehow, this touched me. "So," he asked, "what would you like for breakfast?"

"Soup?" I croaked.

"Done." He got on the horn and mumbled. "Anything else?"

"Water."

He snapped to like a soldier, filling a glass to the brim before setting it at my side.

"What else? Entertainment?"

"You gonna sing?"

"Heaven forbid! How 'bout the radio? Catch the morning news?"

"No thanks. I might be on it."

"You would be," Errol growled, "if Manly wasn't a thug. How'd a bird like that get to where he is?"

"Probably has something on Lenski. Many somethings."

There was a knock on the door. Errol greeted a teenage kid, then passed him some coins. I craned up my head. Chicken soup! From Greenblatt's! Not to mention a bagel loaded with corned beef.

"Errol, you didn't have—"

"I wanted to. You're the only one who really cares about me. And I'll spend the rest of my life trying to pay you back."

Something got in my eye. I blinked.

"That's a two-way street, my friend. Before you came, my best friend was Ma. Pretty pathetic, huh?"

"You could have friends, Nicky. You could be all the rage. Only thing is—you don't want to."

I sighed, rolling onto my good hip. When I opened my eyes, someone tall was standing over me. Bill!

"Hiya," I said softly. "Did I come up in the morning meeting?"

"Nope. Errol called and I came as quick as I could. Nicky, you all right?"

"I'm leadfree, if that's what you mean."

"Nicky, your job is getting too dangerous. Maybe you should go back to the LAPD."

I squinted up at his eyes. Was he on the level?

"And do what?" I asked. "Watch over the Greyhound?"

He sighed, taking a seat on the bed.

"It's just—"

"Don't sweat it, Bill; I've got Errol here to protect me. And he's more than just a pool toy."

Bill looked slightly relieved.

"True." He grabbed hold of my arm like he was scared I'd disappear. "Hate to bring up a sore subject, but . . . did you see who shot you?"

"Nope. Only heard the gat."

Bill leaned forward.

"We should bring in the force."

"*No!*" I shouted. "I like all my shoes 'cause they're not made of cement!"

He frowned.

"Manly?"

"Who else? He says his boys will care take of it. Maybe they will. And solve this whole damn case."

Just thinking it put me squarely back in the dumps.

"Well, black-and-white's waiting," he said. "Better get back." I nodded. "I'll come by as much as I can. See you tonight?"

I smiled.

"I suspect I'll be here. And, Bill, thanks. Please don't tell my mother—she'll smother me in sauce!"

"Sure, Nicky."

He gave me a soft kiss before he backed out the door.

"What a dreamboat!" Errol sighed.

"You want him?"

"Of course not! I meant for *you!* You know . . . by your age, most of the stars are married."

"And trading partners like stock shares."

"Fine. You got me there. But what about you and Bill? Don't you ever want to get hitched?"

"You *have* been talking to Ma!" I cried. "That's all I need—two *ficcanaso!*"

"Huh?"

"Yentas! Busybodies! Trying to play Cupid!"

"Ease off. You'll hurt yourself. I just think you two make a perfect pair."

"You've seen too many movies."

"Only one, but I've *heard* a lot. And when boy meets girl—"

"NO! I will not have my love life reduced to a Mammoth musical!"

Errol threw up his claws. I assumed I wasn't being a very patient patient.

The next week passed so slowly I thought I was going backwards. Christ, I was bored! Errol was sweet, of course, ordering in Chinese, burgers, deli, and Italian. He made breakfast each morning, dancing and humming showtunes. Bill came by when he could, but I think even he was ready for me to rise from my bed. The studio doc, per orders, showed up every day, checking my side.

"How's it look, Doc?"

"Much better. Another two weeks of bedrest—"

"Fat chance." Both Errol and Martin stared down at me as I swept the bedsheets aside. "I've got a case to crack. And if I don't get back to it, someone else could float by on that lake."

"Who do you think shot Tony?" Errol asked.

I shook my head.

"I know as much as you do."

"More importantly—who shot *you?*"

I sat up, crossing my arms.

"Might be the same bird, might not. That's what we need to find out."

Errol mimicked me by folding his claws.

"You should listen to Doc Martin."

"For all I know, he only plays one onscreen."

"I resent that!" Martin cried. Then he shrugged. "It's your funeral, Miss Forenza. I can't force you to take it easy."

Shaking his head sadly, he clicked his black bag closed, picked it up slowly, and left.

"Best Supporting?" I asked Errol.

"Nicky, this isn't a gag. I know you're tough so you don't have to prove it to me. Why not take a couple more days—make sure you're fit for duty?"

Despite his concern, I glowered.

"I've lain around long enough. While I'm playing Snow White, the killer is getting away."

"Suit yourself." Errol sighed. He knew me too well to argue. "Where to now?"

"I'm not sure. In the meantime, let's hit Pink's. If I don't have a chill dog soon, I may just shoot myself."

Chapter 40
A Yes, a No, and a Maybe

Three chili dogs later, I was still flummoxed, but I did feel better. *When all else fails,* Ma always said, *don't forget there's food.*

I thought about all the suspects we'd considered and then discarded: the Felize dame, Westcott, McSweeney, Wellman, Powell. So many big names we could easily make our own movie. Somehow, this didn't help. I sighed all the way down Melrose with Errol, catching sight of the old RKO.

At least one *bad guy,* I thought, *is cooling his heels behind bars.* But somewhere in the city was a bird with a gun and a grudge. I had to nab him before another sop died. *Or,* I thought, got *shot like me.* What I knew from the cops' ballistics: my shooter carried a Luger. This was screwy since most of them went to soldiers. Soldiers who were German. This conjured an image of Freida. Was she more than a bombshell? Maybe she threw the bomb. Despite the persistent sun, I shivered. Had I gotten into a jam *way* above my pay grade?

Still, I refused to be quiet. There were only three of us—dame PI's—in the *entire state,* and I'd be ashamed if I let the other two down.

"C'mon, Errol," I told him, turning back toward La Brea. "Now that we've had brain food, let's try to puzzle this out!"

But even walking for the next hour yielded exactly bupkis. Defeated, we climbed into the Ford and I drove to the office. Once inside, Errol snapped on the radio, entranced by *Stars Over Hollywood*. After I'd slumped past him, the phone rang.

"I'll get it!" I cried, picking up from my office. "Oh, Bill. I've got good news. I've risen from my deathbed."

His voice crackled over the line.

"You think that's smart, Nicky?"

"I'd say the dumb part was getting shot in the first place."

He chuckled.

"Well, since you're on the mend, what say I come by tonight and take you out to a fancy meal?"

"That would be lovely."

"I'm talking Thrifty's. Better take out The Dress."

"Ha! See you later."

I walked back to my joint, my still-bandaged side twitching slightly. Ignoring it, I had a cup of joe to wash down Pink's then got ready for my date. I picked up the phone to call Errol, telling him where I'd be. I sniggered since he'd turned into my Ma!

Once Bill showed up at my door, I threw my arms around his neck. He was still in uniform, and if I were a sap, I just might have swooned.

Since it was close, we walked over to Thrifty's and waited for two empty seats. Once they opened up, we plopped ourselves down on swivel chairs.

"Two coffees, please," I told the girl behind the counter.

"Well?" Bill asked. "Now that Powell's out, anyone else come to mind?"

I shook my head.

"Not one," I sighed into my mug. "One murder's bad enough, but *four?* I don't think Mr. Lombardo ever came up against *that.*"

"I understand," said Bill, "Guiseppe made his dough taking snaps of cheating dames."

"And casanovas," I reminded.

"True. So what do you have so far?"

"Well . . . I have what I think are four murders: Felize, Alexander, Haskel, and McGee. They all worked for Mammoth. They sometimes worked together, and they'd been around forever. Plus, before all this nonsense, Hughley is iced by Goldstein. Is there a connection with Mammoth? Frankly, I tend to think not. We've scratched *Iron Horse*—which means McSweeney, Marion, and Wescott are clean. Ditto Weller and Powell—I'm convinced they didn't do it. Johansson was almost a stiff and I've joined her in that status."

"What about Manly?"

"He wants me off the case—he's made that pretty clear. But even with his connections, why would he kill his employees? That would be bad for business and requires too much coverup. And I think Lenski is on the up and up. He's head of the biggest studio: if he were ever caught, it would be the scandal of the decade. Bigger even than Powell and Carole Lansing."

Bill swiveled toward me.

"You knew?"

"I do live in Hollywood."

"Where does that leave you?" he asked.

"Squat in the middle of nowhere." I half-heartedly ordered a sandwich: I was still pretty full after Pink's. "You're a cop," I said. "Tell me—what am I missing?"

Bill dug into his burger.

"What about Felize?" he asked.

"He's dead."

"Not him—the Frau. She seems to be everywhere, and I wonder: What's her game?"

"She likes actors," I said, "and she's moving her way up the ladder. She doesn't miss poor Larry but would sure miss his insurance. She lives in the Valley, and thinks she's more swell than she is. To me, she's just a fringe dweller aching for attention."

Bill gave me a smile.

"You're as good as the FBI."

"That's a sore spot with me."

"Sorry."

"Anything else?" asked the counter girl, eyeing Bill up and down.

"No thanks. We have enough—of *everything*."

She huffed her way down the counter as I turned to Bill.

"Do you have to be such a dreamboat?" I asked.

"Can't help it," he grinned. "It's all those Swedes in the woodpile."

Once we had finished, Bill dug for some coins.

"Please," I said, "let me. I'm not on contract, but Lenski is paying me well."

"And wound my male pride? Not a chance!"

Even though his tone was light, I saw he looked all nerves.

"You all right? I asked.

"I know this isn't the perfect place—"

"Thrifty's? I like their food."

He folded his hands on the counter.

"No quarrel there. That is . . . we're both so busy, you on this case and me on the force, there never seems to be a good time."

What is he getting at? I wondered. *Were we playing a game, and I was the hot potato?*

"There's never a good time, I guess."

I put down my sandwich, motioning for the girl to wrap it up.

"Oh. I didn't know you saw it like that."

Get on with it, I thought. *Recite me that 'Dear John' letter...*

"Did you think a garden of roses would make it better?" I asked.

Now he started to smile.

"That's why I like you, Nicky. You shoot straight from the shoulder."

I couldn't have been more confused if he'd yelled, "Look! A Martian!"

"Bill." My breath hit my trembling hands. "We've never pulled any punches. Just be square with me"

Lord, how I would miss him! And I thought what we had was real.

"Sure, Nicky," he said, taking a breath. "Ever since we first met, I knew you were something special. Not like the rest of the dames batting their lashes at me." *Where was this going?* I waited for the "but to drop." "Then, at Phillipe's, you knocked me for sixes. And the more time I spend with you—" he tried to smile, "—the more time I *want* to spend with you." *As friends?* "That's why, Nicky, even though the setting's not aces, I want to ask you to marry me." Some unseen force pinned me against my stool. "You keep on with your business, and I'll keep on with mine. Who knows? Maybe someday, we'll work together."

I think I forgot to blink. *Poor sop!* He looked so hopeful in his starched uniform, his eyes trying to tell me what his mouth could not. He reached down with a shaky hand to withdraw from his pocket a small, velvety case.

"No," I said, refusing the box like it contained a grenade. Bill looked crushed. "That is, not 'no' to your proposal. Just . . . maybe, and not right now."

He exhaled, withdrawing the box.

"I don't mean to push you. I'll wait as long as I have to."

"Dear Bill," I murmured, leaning in to kiss his cheek. "I can't make that kind of decision with this case like a Sword of Damocles."

"I understand. I'll shelve it until you're ready. Just let me know when that is."

I nodded, a wet film over my eyes. Once I dragged myself from the counter, I heard Bill trudging behind.

I got the distinct impression he would *not* be staying over.

Chapter 41
Glamor Is What She Sells

I got through the night—barely. Bill had dropped me in the lobby, and I couldn't say I blamed him. I'd just refused his proposal—despite my "maybe"—and thought he might need time to lick his wounds.

God knows that *I* did.

Errol was no dumbbell. He knew something was up. The next morning, as he rose from the couch, he eyed me cooly.

"What is it?" he asked.

"Nothing," I muttered, smelling the phantom aroma of coffee as I shuffled toward the pot.

"Sure. And I'm Errol Flynn."

"Just drop it, all right?"

"Something happened," he said, stepping into his suit. He folded his wings neatly through the gaping holes. "When you got back here, you looked like you'd failed a screentest."

I laughed. Even now, Errol could make me perk up.

"It has nothing to do with the movies. I'll tell you soon, I promise."

He shook his head, causing his tan spikes to flop.

"Keeping dope from your partner? What would Ellery say?"

"Probably to dummy up." Errol raised his claws. He knew when he'd been licked. "Let's scram," I said.

"To where?"

"Mammoth. Figure it's about time to check in with the boss."

He nodded.

"I can't wait to walk to his desk. Think we need track shoes?"

I grinned as we made our way out to the Ford where I slid behind the wheel. Once we got to the north gate, my old friend slipped me a pass.

How long has he been there? I wondered. *Before the invention of sound?*

It wasn't long until we got to Tara—uh, Thalberg.

Inside, it was the same dance. The snooty dame in the lobby; the reluctant call upstairs. Then, a gleaming lift and its attendant depositing us close to Heaven. Of course, a guard waited, unlocking the sacred space with a nod. We treaded expensive carpet on the way to Lenski's office.

"You're back?"

I saw the new assistant still hadn't developed manners. I decided to give her some.

"Look, sweetheart," I said not so sweetly, "I work *directly* for your boss. And what I'm doing is of great importance to him. So maybe you'd like to show a little respect?"

I couldn't help it. I was Italian.

The blonde attempted a smile: not convincing, but better. She buzzed Lenski and I heard a muffled growl, "Okay."

The wood doors opened and as Errol and I walked forward, I wished I had those track shoes. The two lions abutting his desk looked like they wanted to bite.

"Well?" asked Lenski, chomping down on a cigar. It must have been Cuban, since even the smoke smelled good.

"Mr. Lenski, we thought it was time to update you on where we are so far." He nodded, paying attention even as he scanned some thick papers. Then I got to Manly. This caused the studio head to look up. "Mr. Lenski, if you could call off your bulldog . . ."

He nodded.

"Not to worry, he'll go to Havana. Loves the casinos and the broads."

"Thanks. Also, I wanted to pick your brain. No one knows Mammoth like you."

He chuckled.

"Not even Sam Goldfish. Wanted Mammoth named after him! Now he's on Poverty Row."

"Mr. Lenski, if I may: is there anyone else at the studio whom you feel you can't trust?"

"Of course!" he yelled, nearly springing out of his chair. "Do you know how many Reds are on my payroll?"

"No, sir, but the man who tried to kill me carried a Luger."

He crushed out his cigar.

"Not the Krauts again!" He put his head in his hands. "We have more than you think—fled from the war, and all that. Freida Braun is the biggest."

"You had mentioned Hitler hates her?"

"Oh yes. She goes back there and she won't end up in a bunker. Still . . . there's something off about her friend—von Heimlick, von Hussey—"

"Von Heinrich," I said.

Lenski nodded.

"He's one strange duck. Doesn't say much, but it wouldn't surprise me if there's a flag under his bed." He glared. "And it's red and black."

"Hmmm," I said. "Any proof?"

"Not that I know of. But would he run around killing loyal Americans?" He shrugged. "That I can't answer."

This left me stunned. *Had I got this all wrong? Were the murders connected by world events, and not some personal grudge?*

I glanced at Errol, whose face told me he was thinking the same.

"Mr. Lenski . . ." My mind whirled. "Any chance we could talk to Braun? Is she on the lot today?"

"No. She's making a rare appearance. At Bullock's Wilshire. And it better be mobbed!"

"Thanks," I said, motioning to Errol it was time to go. He followed me out toward the now transformed blonde.

"Goodbye, Mr. and Mrs. Forenza," she chirped. "It was a pleasure to see you."

"I'll bet," I muttered to Errol as we laughed our way to the elevator. The attendant inside was not amused.

We clambered back to the Ford, and after waving goodbye to my guard friend, I took Culver, Venice, and Pico, then hung a left on Wilshire. The closer we got to Bullock's, the denser the traffic became. Was all these folks trying to get to Freida? For her—and Lenski's—sake, I hoped so.

I finally got into the lot, waiting behind a Caddy for a valet—*in livery!*—to run up and take the old girl. I looked up at the giant department store. It was a doozy: a high tower topped by copper as tall as the Empire State (what did I know?) framed by small jagged stories ready to soar into the future. We came to a line of mainly women snaking around the building. Waiting for Freida? An excited matron in front of us let go of a shouted, "Yes!"

What was the German's appeal, I wondered, *to all these dowdy women in their outrageous hats?* Freida was a glamour-puss—she had an amazing figure (those legs!)—and made no secret of her bedcapades. She flirted with everyone—not just men—hoarse, sultry voice filled with longing, especially when she sang. That was enough for these women slowing wending their way toward her.

I let the word slip abut Errol and *Fire and Fame,* causing a sort of twitter. We slogged past gleaming displays crowned by a chandelier. The elevators—our only way up—made me feel a bit let down. I'd always wanted to ride on an escalator. Oh well.

Finally, we reached a foyer more like sultan's palace, its red Persian carpets strewn among potted palms. We made it to a tearoom which wasn't exactly cozy. The chairs were backed with rattan, the ceiling fixtures forming a line as straight as a platoon's. Curtains draped the wall, with tasteful vases of flowers placed on every table.

This was, I thought, *as far from Jane Austen as you could get.*

I saw LAPD blue, bulls shifting their eyes as if they expected a riot. Publicists clutched clipboards, hovering like hungry seagulls.

"What do we say when we get to her?" Errol whispered in my ear.

"Not sure. Talk about von Heinrich?"

Errol surveyed the line ahead.

"Fat chance. We'll be lucky to get in a 'Hi!'"

Just as my feet started aching, I saw, through the hats, the outline of shapely legs. They were perched on heels as tall as the tower outside. They belonged to a woman who stood on a wide raised podium, flanked by guards and handlers. Of course. Even her legs were stars.

"Hello, hello, welkommen, so good to zee you! Sank you for coming."

We'd moved up to third in line. I have to confess, my nerves were on edge. That's why I grabbed what passed for Errol's elbow.

"Miss Braun," I breathed, as we stood at her feet like apostles. "My friend is shooting at Mammoth, and we were right in front of you at the Chinese premiere. *Guns N' Ammo.*" I hoped I'd got that right.

"How charming!" She gave me a sultry look which frankly made me weak. "And vat do *you* do?"

This was it.

"I'm a private detective and I'm working for Mr. Lenski."

At her boss' name, she straightened.

"Sehr gut! He is a *charming* man."

I had to swat Errol's arm to keep him still.

"Indeed. You see, we're on a case for him. And he was just wondering: Have you noticed anything strange about your friend Mist—uh, Herr von Heinrich? Any recent change in behavior!"

She frowned along with the women behind us.

"Hmm." she thought, removing her hands from her hips. "Vell, he *is* a strange one. Alvays so bitter."

"About the war?" I asked.

She gave a throaty laugh.

"Oh no! He hates Hitler as much as me. But . . . you see, he's been angry since the Talkies came."

"Put him out of business?"

"In a manner of speaking. You zee, his gwreat silent masterpiece *Gwreed* was cut down from six hours to two." She sighed. "He never directed again. Now, he is doing the acting."

"Where?" I asked curtly.

"Oh, he is on dat new picture, za one vith the name of the street? It's shooting at Mountain."

I felt the kind of shock that must have powered Tesla.

"Miss Braun, I can't thank you enough! I'll tell Mr. Lenski."

Hands back on hips, she bestowed a dazzling smile, and even a wink at Errol.

"Alvays wedy to help the boss."

As Errol and I joined the line to get out, I began to put things together.

Chapter 42
Barbarians at the Gate

F eeling buoyed, I gave the valet a quarter as he handed over the Ford.

"Thank you!" he chirped, moving on to the next jalopy. I must have been that young once.

"I take it," said Errol, stooping to get in, "our next stop is Mountain Pictures?"

"Spoken like a true PI."

Once we got out of the lot, I took Wilshire past Korea Town, hung a right on Wilton, and finally, a left on Melrose.

"It's 5555," Errol said.

I gave him a smile. He truly was the best.

Now came the hard part. I pulled the old girl to a stop by the wrought-iron black gates of Mountain. Classy. With effort, I cranked down my window.

"Excuse me," I said to the guard, who was old and looked crochety. "It's imperative I get to the set of a picture—the one with the name of a street."

"*Sunset Blvd?* Mr. Billy don't like no visitors. That is a closed set."

I opened my bag to flash my license.

"I'm a PI working for Mr. Lenski. I'm trying to get the dope on a series of murders at Mammoth. I'm sure you don't want one here."

The old guy snorted.

"Some people will do *anything* to get on a lot. Listen, sister, leave the stories where they belong—in the pictchas."

I pressed on.

"Can you perhaps make a call? How 'bout to the head of the studio?"

"Zuck Adolph," said Errol.

"Sure, let me do that." The guard mimed talking on the horn.

"'Mr. Adolph, there's some dippy dame who wants to get on the set. And she's with a dragon. No, sir, no one called in a pass. What's that you say? Throw her out on her keister? Consider it done!"

He smirked, index finger miming a U-turn. This wasn't going to work. We'd never get through the gate.

"I wonder if there's a back entrance," I mumbled, noting the stiff barbed wire atop the fence.

"If there is," said Errol, "it's guarded. Brother, this place seems more buttoned up than Mammoth."

"Well," I told him," Mammoth's as big as Lockheed. People must come and go all day."

"Plus," said Errol, "this joint makes 'serious pictures.' They have all the top directors, and boy, do they know it!"

I nodded.

Our search for another way in yielded zip. And all that barbed wire didn't look friendly.

"Let's go back to the office," I said. "Put our heads together." After a short but silent drive, we took the stairs up. After unlocking the door, I sighed. "I see there's no lines around the block."

"You don't need new clients," said Errol. "Not until this case is cracked."

I sighed.

"Okay." I motioned him into my office, sinking into my chair. "First question. If it *is* von Heinrich, do you think he had help?"

Errol hung to the back of my guest chair.

"My instincts says no. Whoever he'd find would have to be as nuts as him."

"You'd be surprised," I said, "what people will do for a C-note."

"Not at all. I've been around long enough to know everyone here speaks dough. Still, *murder?* He'd have to find a punk like Eddie. And would even that hood take the risk of blipping four birds in public?"

I leaned back.

"Probably not. And from what Freida said, her friend is low on his luck. Where would he get the clams to pay off an Eddie?"

"Good point," said Errol. "Guess that's why you're in charge." I barely managed a grin.

"Then . . . assuming von Heinrich acted alone: How do we get to him before he moves on to somebody else? That gate is like a drawbridge! Short of renting a plane from Clover Field—"

"Nicky," Errol cut in. "What does a plane do?"

I fought the urge to slap him . . . gently, of course.

"They take off, they fly, they land."

"Exactly."

"Save the puzzles for Ellery Queen! Exactly what are you getting at?!"

"You've seen me use *these*—" he pointed to the thin wings folded across his back—"already. Forget we dragons do more than just breathe fire? Sister—WE FLY! And *that's* how we get into Mountain."

"Errol," I said, "I could kiss you!"

"Please don't," he grimaced.

I started to pace.

"We wait for night and fly into the studio. Then we get on the set and stop von Heinrich from killing his next victim!"

"That would probably be Lily Swan."

"The old Silent star?"

"She's top of the bill on *Sunset Blvd.*"

"Oh boy." I steadied my hands. "May his part be so big he won't have time to ice her today."

Errol grinned.

"You—a cockeyed optimist?"

"What choice do I have?"

It was a long afternoon which threatened never to end. I spent it sipping Bacardi while Errol turned on the box. He better be picking up pointers from Ozzie—or Harriet.

The L.A. sun left reluctantly. It was 4:47. Good thing we weren't by the equator.

I watched Errol strip off his suit.

"Slippery," he explained. "That cheap Woolworth stuff would tumble you like the laundromat."

I nodded, slipped on my jacket, and followed him out until we both stood in the lobby.

"Where do we . . . take off?" I asked, trying to steady my voice.

"Doesn't matter," he said. "Just someplace we can't be seen."

"How about . . . the top of this building?"

He shrugged.

"As long as we can get to the roof."

"We stowed away on a yacht, remember?"

He gave me a grin as we crammed back into the lift. I'd never been higher than 2 and now he pushed 13. Just our luck. Once we got up there, we searched for a roof exit. Errol was the one who found it—a tight cubbyhole with short stairs. He struggled to fit his bulk through as we both clambered up concrete.

Hollywood. From up here, it truly was magical, bathed in neon, autos snaking in alternate lines of white and red. I had it admit it: This was my town.

Errol padded to the edge of the roof, trying out his thin but strong wings. Up close, I noticed they were lined with diaphanous veins. I gulped. There hadn't been many times when I'd turned chicken—not on the job, at least. But a nighttime flight on a dragon over the bustle of Hollywood? I wished I had that Bacardi.

The fear found its way to my stomach with the speed of a P-38.

What was I doing? I wondered. *Had I, like von Heinrich, fallen off the train for the sane?*

"Errol," I whispered.

He turned.

"Wha-what should I do?"

"Just hang on like before. Sit like a lady and grab hold of my spikes." Then he lay low, going down on all fours. "Get on," he said. "Production and killers don't wait."

Chapter 43
Hollywood Magic

I walked toward him, shaking, then swung my legs over his back like I was riding side-saddle. Since I wore a skirt, I pretty much had no choice. Through its thin wool, I felt the hard surface of scales prickling my backside and making me totter. Still, I steadied myself as Errol spread his wings, half reptile and half angel. He clawed the roof's ledge briefly, then let go, jumping out over Hollywood Boulevard. I screamed, grabbing some neck spikes, and closing my eyes.

"Easy," he groaned. "You've got a grip like King Kong. Don't you know I won't let you fall?"

"Yes?" It was more of a question.

"A dragon can always be trusted. Not that I've known any others."

I felt him climb, the swoosh of his wings creating a sharp breeze.

"No," I whimpered.

Errol turned his head to face me.

"How you like the view?"

"Can't. Say. Only dark.

I felt the tremor of his chuckle.

"Nicky, open your eyes! It's beautiful!"

I wished I had the moxie to lift my lids on my own. Since I wasn't, I used fingers, making sure not to look down. Before me were all four horizons from Hollywood. From this height, everything blazed: shop signs and club names; Alpha Beta and Thrifty. I saw a premiere at the Egyptian, klieg lights blinding as they circled the sky and us. I could imagine the crowd cheering; the sizzle of flashbulbs and stars arriving in limos. Daring to look up, I saw real stars above, their light a pale reflection compared to those below. LIGHTS. CAMERA. ACTION. I blinked at a building with columns crowned by sphinx heads, and stairs which sloped like a pyramid beckoning patrons inside.

China. Egypt. Latin America, I thought. That was Hollywood in a nutshell. It hijacked other cultures and bent them to its will, only bigger and brighter. Was that wrong? Facing with the town from on high, I didn't think so.

But such bliss could never last. As Errol began to drop, I saw the wrought-iron gates which had barred our earlier entry. Now, we simply flew over them, and like a brat, I wanted to thumb my nose, but there was no one to see me.

Errol started to glide and we both bent to search the lot below. Mountain wasn't as big as its namesake, so it wasn't hard to spot night shooting in its farthest corner. The unnatural lights were like a homing signal and Errol set down—with care—at the side of a full-sized pool. Which only an actor would swim in.

Happily, the pool was spared from lights—it just sat in the semi-darkness, waters still. But the set of a mansion was lit like the sun: white, with long, curving steps, it was nearly engulfed by crew. One guy in a suit must be the director since he was shouting. "Wild Billy." I knew he was some kind of legend, but not that he was from Europe until I heard him speak.

"Quiet! Now. we do an establishing shot of Norma coming out. Remember, she's gone bananas and has just shot the writer. Pull back and zoom in as she moves. I want the feel of tragedy, dark noir at its height. *Extras below the stairs!* You are to stay perfectly still."

Errol pointed up at a lone figure, her head wrapped in a turban.

"That's Lily Swan," he whispered.

But where was von Heinrich?

Billy called for "ACTION!" leading to a wooden thwack. Swan began her long descent, arms moving like tangled snakes, long nails menacing. I stepped back, frantically gesturing to Errol. I pointed out von Heinrich, posture impossibly straight, clothed in a butler's uniform, monocle still in place. He was waiting for Swan at the bottom of that staircase.

"This is it," I hissed. "Watch his hands!"

We both stood there breathless, just a few yards away, until the ex-director reached inside his coat.

"I'm ready for my close-up, Mr. DeMille," Swan purred, as big as the silver screen when she contorted her body. Errol crouched on concrete, prepared to launch himself forward, when the German's hand emerged, wrapped around an old Luger. Errol lunged for Swan, von Heinrich pointed the gun—but not at her, at DeMille, playing himself!

Like a reliable potboiler, everything happened at once: Errol blocked DeMille, taking the bull for him, then stumbled back a few steps to fall into the pool.

"ERROL!" I yelled, jumping in after him. I swam to his prostrate face, face down and floating in the deep end. With effort, I flipped him over, but was distracted by the scene playing out on those steps.

"DeMille! You can't escape me!" von Heinrich screamed, his face a hideous mask. "You ruined my masterpiece! You cut it into shreds,

making a mockery of my genius. And now, it's time to pay! Ungrateful dog!"

I looked up to Swan, who stood midway on the long staircase, the madness in "Norma's" eyes replaced by genuine fear.

"Heinrich," she called. "Don't do this! We can find *Greed's* negative! We can restore its glory!"

Whether she was acting or not, I couldn't tell, but it gave me a chance to pound Errol's stomach with all my strength.

"Errol!" I screamed, *"don't you dare die on me now!"*

I realized I sounded like a three-hankie picture, but what else could I do? My partner and best friend was dying!

He coughed. I pounded harder. He sputtered, a tiny flame extinguished in a cloud of black smoke.

"Can't . . . flame," he gasped. "Nicky—up to you!"

I reached in my bag—pulled out the damp .38. A shot rang out from somewhere. The Luger tumbled to concrete. Then the shrill of a siren, a black-and-white screeching its brakes. A uniformed cop jumped out: *Bill!*

He ran to bend over von Heinrich, checking the German's pulse. When he rose, he shook his head.

The film crew began to stir. I swam to the edge of the pool, pulling myself out. Errol just stood in the deep end, his back claws hitting bottom.

"Thank you!" DeMille approached me, shaking my soggy hand.

"Oh yes," said Swan, descending to meet us. In her turban and glittering gown, she looked every inch the star.

"What," the cameraman asked, "the hell happened?"

I took a deep breath, shaking out my hair.

"As I see it," I said, "von Heinrich left us a clue, but we basically ignored it." I turned to Errol. "That note on the cutter's body: 'Don't be greedy.' Every murder that's happened has to do with *Greed.*"

Even Errol looked confused. I turned to DeMille. "I assume you produced that picture? And that Larry Felize, Tony Alexander, Wes Haskell, and Patrick Magee all worked on it?"

The legendary showman thought.

"I do remember most of my pictures. And yes, those names are familiar from the early days."

"I take it Swan was the star? Along with Ingrid Johansson?"

"That's right," said the producer.

"I was on the wrong track all along: foxing around love affairs and not thinking of the Business. But that's what it's all about: Hollywood. Not the stars, but a single lost picture." I shrugged at Errol. "We thought it was *Iron Horse,* but we were wrong. The culprit was here and at Mammoth, hiding in plain sight."

"But-but why," DeMille asked, "go after the crew? It was my decision to make the cuts—and Lenski's."

"He couldn't get to Lenski," I said. "Not with Manly in the wings. So he took it out on the little guys: if they'd worked on the picture, they were marked for murder."

"Thank God Ingrid and Lilly weren't harmed!" cried DeMille.

And me, I thought.

"It wasn't for lack of trying."

We all just stood there, the entire crew immobilized. The mood was solemn—except for Wild Billy.

"Goddammit!" he cried. "We'll have to retake that shot!"

"It's beats your star getting shot," I said.

"Sure, sure." He gestured Swan back up the stairs. "Everyone, take their places!"

Bill had the presence of mind to drag Heimrich out of sight. God forbid he should be in the frame.

These Hollywood types, I thought. *They act like real murder is only make-believe.*

I walked toward the waterlogged Errol.

"You okay?" I asked.

"Swell. Like a pill can puncture *this* hide."

I reached out to pat his claw, Above us, Swan wiped away tears, and I could swear they were real.

"Poor, deluded man," she said.

I couldn't share her feelings: not after being on the business end of that Luger.

"Well, it's over," I breathed, walking toward to Bill to put an arm around him. "Thanks for getting here so quick."

"I did nothing. This one belongs to you." He bent to give me a kiss.

"Can we get on with it?" Billy huffed, scrambling up the camera crane.

As he prepared the shot, DeMille strolled over to Errol.

"What's your story?" he asked.

"I'm on *Flame and* . . . oh hell, I'm really a dragon."

DeMille cocked a heavy eyebrow, surveying my soaking friend.

"Say," he said, "how'd you like to be in pictures?"

Made in United States
Troutdale, OR
03/18/2024

18559553R10146